OVERRULED

City Romance Book One.

POPPY BREEZE

Ebook ISBN: 978-1-7384869-1-5
Paperback ISBN: 978-1-7384869-0-8

CONTENTS

CHAPTER ONE

The sound of the traffic grew louder and louder, and a wave of angry voices began to mix with the equally-angry revving of overheating engines. Fia began to realise that it was getting close to rush hour; that she'd been staring at clothes for half a day, and that she'd had enough. It was definitely now time to go home. Shopping wasn't exciting for her at the best of times, and the pressure of a deadline made it torture; she was tired, and her feet hurt. She wondered how long it would take to get back to her apartment in all this traffic.

"The shops will be closing soon, surely?" she called over the sound of a car waiting at the traffic lights, its roof down and music blaring.

"Late night opening," was the only reply from

her friend Louella, who was studying the contents of another shop window, swaying in time to the drum and bass coming from the car stereo. The driver blew her a kiss as the lights changed to green and he sped away. She completely ignored him.

Fia walked over to see what she was looking at through the window glass, which was coated in a fine layer of pollution. It was very dirty. She felt hot and dirty too. Her hair was an angry snarl that pulled at her scalp and was starting to give her a headache. It was time to call it a day, before she just curled up into a ball and went to sleep on the pavement.

"Oh no," said Louella, making eye contact in the glass. "Not yet. And it's your fault if you're tired – you should have called me earlier in the day, when you first started floundering. You need at least one decent business suit. I didn't pull all these strings to get you a job interview, just for you to mess it up right at the beginning. Come on, we're going in."

Fia followed her through the door, which closed behind them with a polite snick. It was almost silent inside; there were no other customers at this time of day, just rows and rows of suits in expensive fabrics that whispered to her as she ran her fingers over them. She flipped over a price tag, her eyebrows rising at the number of zeros.

"I can't afford these, Lou!" she said. "No wonder we're the only ones in this place - have you seen the prices?"

Louella stood back and made a show of looking Fia up and down, taking her all in. She started with the knotted blonde hair that stood up in all directions and carried on past her glasses with the wonky arm that were drifting to the left. She ran her eyes down over the bobbly hoodie and the yoga pants, where they came to rest accusingly on her faded tennis shoes.

"The price doesn't matter at this point. We've run out of time, and you need this job. I know you don't see yourself as a receptionist, but it pays well. And we would be working together, which would be amazing, right?

Fia nodded reluctantly. "Right," she agreed.

"But you have to dress the part," Louella continued. You'll be the first face of the law firm, Fia. You need to look..."

"Reliable," said the sales assistant, clicking towards them on the polished floor. Fi wondered whether her heels were damaging it. "You need something that looks glamorous enough for clients to engage with you, and responsible enough for them to trust you with their secrets. This," she paused as she absorbed the interesting sight of Fia, "Won't do at all. Good afternoon, Ms Louella. It's good to see you again."

Her judgemental friend smiled. "Hello. My

friend here needs a makeover, please. We're on a tight schedule. The interview is tomorrow morning."

Fia dropped the price tag with a sigh. She had been friends with Louella since nursery school; she knew when to let her win. And after all, she was truly grateful for the job interview. The little amount she'd made in royalties from her children's books hadn't paid any bills in months, and she needed to do something else to make up the shortfall.

Honestly, she really needed to write a new book, but that wasn't happening any time soon. She hadn't been able to bring herself to even *read* any of her stories for a long time. Opening the pages made her heart race, and if she forced herself to start sounding out the words then a panic attack would set in, and she would be useless.

Her agent used to arrange visits for her. Fia would read her books to school children across the country, practicing her delivery on the long train journeys across fields and alongside the ocean. It's a shame they'd all had to be cancelled this year. She loved watching their little eyes widen as they listened to her, and the big smiles on their faces when the happy ending arrived. They were too young to figure out that not all dragons were slain in real life.

But unfortunately, this was real life, and her rent wasn't being vanquished any time soon. The magazines may have named her most promising children's author of the year, but potential alone didn't make money. Maybe Louella was right, and it was time to be more serious, to get a proper job - and this was perfectly embodied in her graceful best friend. Louella seemed perfectly at home in this shop, walking around it like a she owned the place in a sharp grey suit that was exactly the colour of a gun barrel.

She worked for one of the top law firms in the City; JD Bard Associates, and ran the main reception desk in the lobby with poise and experience. Fia had visited her there more than once when they went out to eat lunch together and was more than a little intimidated by the workload. Would she even be able to keep up with her, if she got the job?

Louella didn't entertain this question for a minute. "You'll learn quickly, don't worry. Just relax in the interview and you'll be fine - I trust you! My co-worker is off on maternity leave, so it's only for a year anyway. You'll be back writing kids adventures in no time. But debt-free, which is very important." Louella grinned, swung three jackets free from a low rail and passed them to the waiting assistant. "I'll tell you what. I'll loan you the money for the clothes, but I get to choose them. Deal?"

Fia smiled. "Deal," she said, and succumbed completely. Two sets of manicured hands pushed her gently towards the changing rooms.

The next hour was a whirlwind of smooth fabric. These new clothes were tighter than she was used to, hugging her chest and hips. The sales assistant ran her hands over the skirts, adjusting them so they shaped correctly around her legs. She took her job very seriously, head bowed down as she adjusted her panties so the line didn't show through the skirt. Fia could smell a light flowery perfume on the back of her neck, and wondered what was taking so long. Louella laughed, and tapped the woman lightly on the head, running an admonitory finger down her neck.

"Leave her alone," she whispered in her ear. "I'll get jealous."

The women snapped her into bras made from light lace that lifted her small breasts perfectly together. Her silver necklace dropped into the space between them, the diamond-encrusted 'F' that hung from it vanished completely into her cleavage. She was shimmied into silk blouses that buttoned tight over the top. They brought her cashmere sweaters that she just wanted to stroke on the hangers, and didn't dare to try on. She wore creams and whites and navy blues; cool colours that allowed the light sun-glow from her summer skin to shine. She wore layers of whispered fabrics that seemed to be made of nothing at all. Luckily, they looked solid enough in the floor-length mirror as the two women with her firmly gripped her by the shoulders and twisted her left and right, checking her silhouette from all angles.

Fia hadn't been touched this much for a year. Her skin felt warm, despite the thin layers.

Six shopping bags were packed full before she was back in her gym wear again, and Louella slid her credit card into the reader at the till.

"I'll pay you back with my first pay check," Fia promised, horrified at the total.

"I know you will. And now you have to get the job, so you can't fluff up the interview. See? This was my cunning plan all along."

"And I've given her my friends and family discount," said the shop assistant, with a wink. "Just to persuade you to return any time."

Fia thought she saw a ghost of a wink returned, as her friend smiled.

"Do you mind if I don't come home with you?" Louella asked suddenly. "You should probably get an early night if you want to be fresh for tomorrow, right? We'd end up talking all evening."

"Are you sure I can't drive you back?"

Louella shook her head. "I'll get a taxi, it's fine. And I brought you this – We've gone to so much effort today to dress you for the part, you should have an idea about the current case the partners are working on. You'll have to nail that interview tomorrow." She returned her credit card to her handbag and withdrew a thick envelope. She gave to Fia, who frowned.

"You said you couldn't help me with this. You told me that you signed an NDA-"

"Then get the job, and you'll sign one too. It will be fine. I'm in the mood for breaking a few rules today. And I trust you, Fi. You won't tell anyone else."

Fia doubted cheating was a good start for a new job, but then she looked at the purchases scattered on the floor and thought of their prices, of the emails asking her to pay her bills, and the rent due next month. When she cracked open the top of it, she saw a thick bundle of papers, the headings highlighted in aggressive fluorescent green. Her heart sank. It would take hours to go through it all, and she only had the one night.

"I couldn't get it to you any earlier, and don't ask me where I got it from. At least you'll understand their problems a little bit by tomorrow. I wish you all the best of luck, and I'll be there on the desk in the morning, thinking good vibes. Can you carry all of that yourself?"

Fia sighed, and gently put the envelope into the wide pocket of her hoodie before picking up the bags. They might be big, but they were lighter than air. She wondered for a moment if she would feel naked in these clothes the next day; here was no material to hide behind at the interview at all. Her skin prickled for a moment with nervousness, and she felt cold for the first time that afternoon. She covered it at once with a smile.

"Not a problem," she assured her friend. "I'll burn this after I read it, right? I suppose it would be really embarrassing if I didn't even know about the type of cases you help with. I won't let you down, I promise... shall I leave you here, then?"

"It would be best. You won't waste any time. And I might just have a little look around this place myself, and see if something here fits me. It caught my eye earlier, but I don't want to keep you waiting while I try it on for size."

She trailed one hand gently down the assistant's forearm, capturing another hint of scented moisturiser. Fia could smell it on her as she gave her a quick hug goodbye and walked back into the late dirty sunshine out on the street. The door was closed and locked behind her the very second that she'd squeezed the bags through it, and the sign was immediately flipped to 'Closed'. Fia rolled her eyes and smiled all the way back to the car park. Louella really could hook up anywhere.

Her smile faded as she returned to her car. There was so much to do, and so little time to do it all in - it would take an age to unwrap all of these clothes when she got back, and the weight of the paper in her pocket promised hours of work on its own. Although she had to admit, it would be great to understand more about the owners of the company. Louella had briefly told her about the two cousins who had started J D Bard Associates together in their twenties, with nothing but a small bank loan and big ideas. Their reputation had soared in the last fifteen years, their dream crystalising into the largest and most influential law company in the City. Fia couldn't imagine holding onto that level of self-belief for so long. She hoped the people that worked for them weren't as intimidating.

The bags knocked against her aching legs as she reached her ancient Nissan Micra, and Fia huffed. She'd have to find the energy to do everything from somewhere. Failing the interview was no longer an option; she owed Louella too much to even think about it.

When she located her car on the end of its row, the sight of it caused her already sinking heart to make its way down to the floor and bump into her ankles. She was blocked in by a shiny Mercedes, which someone had abandoned cross-wise over the pedestrian zone, drawn close to her vehicle with barely a millimetre to spare.

This wasn't good. She couldn't leave her parking bay; she couldn't even open the trunk to store her purchases.

"Damn these city drivers," she cursed, kicking

its wheel.

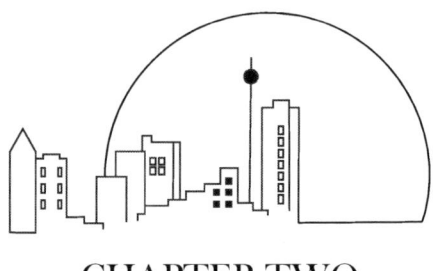

CHAPTER TWO

Fia managed to unlock her driver's door and open it one-handed. She shoved the clothes through the gap to the back, where they lay strewn on the seat, removing the possibility of any use for her rear-view mirror. She then gently closed the door again and walked back round to the Mercedes. She leaned calmly against its wing, crossing her arms as she tapped one tennis-shoed foot. She may have no choice but to wait for the driver to come back, but she would be having words.

She had been scrolling on her phone for twenty-five minutes before a figure approached her, and the first thought that went through her mind was that this man matched his car. He wore dark grey business suit that screamed 'don't touch me'. His shoulders were broad and straight, but held tensely, as though he knew someone was always looking at him. He must have seen her, but he made no eye contact at all as he walked calmly back to his vehicle, swinging a small shopping bag from one nonchalant finger.

"Sure, don't rush," said Fia. "Take your time. I'm happy to wait."

The man looked at her, then. He sighed. "Apologies, I'm sure," he said. "I wasn't long, though. Surely you've only been here for a minute or two?"

He smiled at her. It was charming, with a slight crinkle at the corner of his eyes. Well-practiced. Obviously, this was a smile that worked on a lot of people. He had high cheekbones, she noted. Grey eyes, and dark hair. Was that a hint of silver in it? He looked too young for that. Maybe he had a stressful career. Something that paid well enough for him to buy a stupid, large Mercedes that he used to block in women that had better places to be, and promises to keep. She suddenly didn't feel like humouring him.

"No," she said.

The smile vanished instantly. "Well, I appreciate your patience, then - I had something very important to do, so keeping you waiting for a moment really was the lesser of two evils." He tapped his bag. "Paperwork that had to be delivered. Life or death, I'm sure you understand."

Fia knew that she could be too gentle; her

friends were always calling her a pushover. She usually didn't like confrontation at all, but something about this man had her on edge. She clasped the 'F' on her necklace tightly, and she could feel the diamonds that her brother had chosen digging into her fingers, turning them white. Life or death? She doubted it.

"Life or death," she repeated slowly. "Right - if this was an ambulance, I could understand that; but a businessman is just that - a businessman. I expect the only person benefiting here is yourself, and no -" she cut him off before he could interrupt her, "I really couldn't wait today. I have something important to prepare for. You're not the only person in the world with problems."

"You have something as important, do you? I doubt that. I argue for a living, I know an exaggeration when I hear one."

He tipped his head to one side with these words, and stared at her. Fia was suddenly acutely aware of her messy appearance. She pushed her hair away from her eyes and hunched her shoulders, as if that would hide the wear and tear visible on her hoodie.

"Appearances aren't everything," she muttered.

"Yes, well. If you get off my car, I'll get out of your way."

Fia grinned, and found herself yawning and stretching. "Sorry, it might take me a moment. I've been here so long that my muscles have seized; you'll have to bear with me. Patience is a virtue, as you say."

She eventually stood up straight, rolling her shoulders nonchalantly. The man glared at the wing of the car as she left it, and her eyes widened as she looked back, and saw the dusty curved imprint of her butt cheeks on the side of it. Her yoga pants were dirtier than she expected them to be. Her first instinct was to apologise, but as she saw the judgement in his eyes another wave of anger came over her.

"Wipe that look from your face," she said. "Or I'll sit on your car again. If it has butt prints all over it, people might realise what an asshole you are."

He looked at her incredulously, and snapped his mouth shut as he pulled a set of car keys from his jacket pocket. It was obvious he had given up on the conversation.

Fia opened her own driver's door again and got in, now at the point of frustrated exhaustion. She jammed her key into the ignition and hoped he would take a long time to put his seatbelt on; it would give her time to rev her engine violently while he struggled with it.

But he was too efficient. When she looked up, the Mercedes was gone.

Fia's frustration vanished the following day; she was too much in awe of Louella's place of work. This was a big building. Fia counted at least thirty floors when she looked upwards at the long line of windows stretching away from her and into the sky. The glass doors at the entrance opened automatically as she approached them; sterile, and untouchable. She walked into the wide space of the atrium and took in the shiny tiled floor, the chrome pillars, and the elevators that nestled between the over-arching ornamental orange trees that lived on the other side of the security gates. It was a beautiful space, but severe. Judgement seemed to radiate from every reflective surface.

This wasn't the first time she'd been here of course, but it looked completely different to her today, now she was here for a job interview. She saw Louella sitting behind the reception desk. Her friend didn't wave, but Fia received a professional smile that tipped up at the corners slightly more than it usually would. She was happy to see her, then.

Fia tapped her way over to the desk, making sure that her heels made peaceful, measured clicks against the tiles beneath her. She wasn't in a rush. She was calm, it was fine.

"Hello," she said.

"Hello, said Louella. "Fancy meeting you here." She put a square of plastic on the desk, and pushed it towards Fia with one finger. "I have a security card here for you - it's only valid for today, so don't forget to return it to reception before you leave. The interviews are on the seventh floor, which may be lucky for some. Take the elevator. You'll see some chairs when you get up there, have a seat and wait to be called."

Louella looked very relaxed. Whatever had occurred in the clothes shop, it must have been a very good evening. Fia took the lanyard from her and placed the ribbon of it carefully around her neck.

"Who's interviewing me, do you know?" she asked, a ball of nerves in comparison.

"Darby Bard," Louella said. "He's one of our founding partners. Look as smart as you can and stay as quiet as you can – if you ramble on, you might let him get something on you; it's his career to poke information out of people. Just remember that silence is golden, okay?"

"Okay," Fia said, keeping her answer short. It was best to start now, and get some practice in.

"Darby's the person I asked about interviewing you," Louella continued to explain, "But I never thought he'd see you himself, it's usually someone from the HR department. I was quite flattered that he took my recommendation so seriously."

Fia nodded, and felt the pressure increase

around her lungs. She took a deep breath while she still could.

"And there's the other one, of course. I don't know why they're using his office – he's a nightmare. Be careful of him. He's got a way of cutting you into smaller pieces with just his words. He's-"

But then the clock struck ten, and Louella flapped her arms towards the elevators. Fia was out of time, and it wouldn't be a good idea to be late. She beeped the card against a short metal pillar, and crossed through the security gate. There wasn't an orange out of place on the trees in front of her. Everything in this place was so smart.

She straightened one earring while she waited for the elevator number to reach zero and the doors to open, and realised now that the colour scheme Louella had chosen for her new clothes complemented the building completely. She looked as though she belonged here, as though she'd worked here for years.

If only I had, she thought. Then I'd know my way around this place a little more already. The elevator rose, the doors opened, and their polite ding revealed a space with four identical doors, and four groups of chairs. It was all wool carpet and beige walls that muffled any sound from the rooms beyond them. This was definitely the place to keep a secret.

Fia didn't know which area she should wait in.

In the end, she held her ear to each of the doors to try and hear a voice from inside one of them; at least this would give her an idea that one was occupied. She felt her ear against the coolness of the wood door with her first two tries, and could only hear silence, but at the third one she could hear the faint sounds of a conversation on the other side. She held her breath to reduce the noise on her side even further, and listened.

"...on her way," she heard. "We'll just see if she's any good, then?"

"Why do you need me here for that? I've got an entire case file to read, before the defendant turns up after lunch. This is a complete waste of time-"

"I'll be quick. I'm only doing our receptionist a favour with the interview; we don't need to hire this girl. Don't worry about it."

There was the sound of someone flipping pages. "She's not a good candidate for us. A children's author? She writes little stories – oh God, you know I don't do cute. What were you thinking, agreeing to this?"

"Honestly, I just wanted to use your office. It has such a pretty view."

A short laugh. "Don't try and steal my office, Darby - I'd hate to get cross with you. All right, fine. Just get her in, but I'm taking no part in this - interview her yourself, I'll just sit here."

Footsteps sounded. The handle rattled, and Fia jumped back from the door. She sat in one of the leather seats just as it opened, and breathed out slowly. That was close. Louella would never have forgiven her if she'd ruined her chances this early on. Although by the sound of it, she wouldn't be getting the job anyway. Her shoulders sank.

"Come in, Ms Devlin. We're ready for you now."

Fia looked up to see a friendly face beneath a mass of curly brown hair. It smiled at her, and waved her into the room. She realised that her skirt had stuck to the back of her thighs with nervous sweat, and she pulled it free as she stood up.

"Thank you," she said.

CHAPTER THREE

The curly-haired man who had organised the interview was right; this room had a beautiful view. Soft late-morning clouds surrounded the pinnacles of all the high-rises that stood in rows through the financial district. The busy traffic snaked around the bases of them, and the low-angled sun that shone through the buildings glinted from their bonnets like scales. A shimmer of heat shook upwards from the tarmac, and softened the edges of the architecture. It was going to be another hot day.

Fia was grateful for the air-conditioning unit that was currently playing with her hair, even if it had only cooled the room down by a few degrees. She stood in the path of it for a moment, but she knew she'd stared out of the window for a little too long when she heard a throat clearing behind her.

"Hello, are you with us? Feel free to take a seat at any time," she heard a voice say, "We're over here at the desk when you're ready."

Fia froze. She'd recognised the soft accent at once. Suddenly she didn't want to leave the beautiful view in front of her; she didn't want to turn and look at the new, awful reality inside the room. But the gentle clicking sound of the clock on the wall reminded her that time continued to pass, and she knew she didn't have a choice - and so she twisted round and looked straight into the judgemental grey eyes of the man sitting at the main desk by the window.

Damn it all to hell - it was Mr Mercedes. She waited to be thrown out of the office, for him to demand that she pay the cleaning bill for his car, but the moment didn't come. The two lawyers on the other side of the desk merely continued to sit there in silence until she joined them, and so after another few heartbeats she sat in the empty chair opposite theirs, not knowing what else she could do.

"My name is Darby," said the man with curly hair. "And this is..."

But Fia was finding it hard to concentrate; she was trying to search the face of the man in front of her for a hint of recognition, but he'd only looked up at her briefly before returning to his paperwork. She could barely see an inch of his forehead, no matter how long she stared at him, and there wasn't much emotion in it. Usually, she could tell a lot from a forehead.

After a moment he must have felt her eyes on him, and he looked back up, leaving her to wonder whether her eyes were burning a hole in the top of his head. I hope they are, she thought grimly. I hope it stings.

He didn't seem concerned by her gaze; he merely met her eyes and stared gently back at her. There was no curiosity in it, merely evaluation. He wasn't bothered, then - he didn't seem to remember who she was at all. Maybe he argued with people in car parks every day, and this wasn't enough to make her memorable. He probably blocked cars in all the time. Asshole.

He looked a little older with the morning sun on him. Fine lines were beginning to touch the corner of his eyes. He must force himself to smile a lot for work; Fia couldn't imagine him ever being cheerful on purpose.

The clock on the wall continued to tick, and Darby was still talking. Fia pulled her focus back to him in panic, trying to join back in with his conversation and ignore the problem sitting next to him. There was nothing else she could do, after all. His co-worker either remembered her and this was all a game, or he didn't – and either way, she would have to continue with the interview as though they were complete strangers meeting for the first time.

He was nodding now, agreeing with something Darby had said. Fia nodded along, but she had no clue why she was doing it.

"And so, Ms Devlin. We have your resume here of course, but please do tell us something about yourself," Darby said as he finished his little speech. "We'll learn so much more about you from a chat."

Fia could do this; she'd spun a story in front of an audience before. She'd do it for Louella. She opened up her mouth to speak, but had barely formed the first word when Mr Mercedes interrupted her.

"If it's relevant to our field, of course. I don't have time to listen to every little happy achievement you've made to literature. Stick to the point."

Fia blinked. Didn't she hear him say that he wouldn't get involved, when she listened through the door? Why was he picking on her already?

"Well, my degree *is* in literature," she said slowly, trying to force her mind into gear. "So I'll be able to respond to clients well in writing... and although I haven't worked for a law firm before, I do think I have other skills that would benefit you. I-"

"Great, Darby. She can spell. Surely that's the bare minimum?"

"I also have experience with confidential information, and dealing with emotional people," Fia added quickly, cutting him off in return. "I've worked on the main reception in a hospital-"

A quiet scoff. "This is one of the best law firms in the capital. I hardly think that is remotely comparable to the standard we expect here. And this is only a year-long contract. By the time we train you to our standards you'd be out of here. How can you prove to us that you are worth the bother?"

His grey eyes met her ice blue ones, no hint of a smile in them this time. She knew he'd already made a decision about her future in this building; she'd known it before she walked through the door, and so she decided not to waste her energy arguing with him about it. She just nodded coolly at him, and didn't continue with her speech.

"Do you have any questions for me?" she asked instead.

"Not at all. Your resume was extremely... informative. Darby?"

Darby collected the pages of her resume together and made an effort to look through them before he folded them in half and smiled at her. "Did you enjoy your previous experience as a receptionist?" he asked her.

Fia thought about that for a moment. "Yes," she said, surprising even herself. "I did. I was able to help a lot of vulnerable people. I could make their experience just a little smoother and less complicated. I expect that would be the same here. It doesn't matter whether someone is waiting for a life-changing diagnosis, or preparing for a ruling in court, really. The stress would be the same. I was useful."

"Well then, that's good to know," said Darby, with a polite nod. "I must say, your application came completely from left field, but you've definitely given us something to think about. We'll be in touch when the interviews are closed."

Mr Mercedes said nothing, and drank his coffee. His cufflinks glinted in the sunshine from the window as he raised the cup; they matched the light in his eyes. He noticed her attention on him, and smirked as Fia looked away. She thanked them both for their time, and managed to keep the irony out of her voice before she made her escape back to the elevator.

She was still waiting for it to arrive when she heard laughter coming from the room. Ah, well. She'd always doubted that she'd make the grade to work here, but at least she'd tried her best. And at least the tags were still in all the clothes Louella had paid for; she'd be returning them to the shop that they'd come from soon enough.

Fia examined herself in the shiny chrome of

the doors of the elevator as soon as they shut, cutting off the laughing voices and leaving her safely alone. Her eyes looked twice the size now her hair was out of her face, swept smoothly upwards and twisted into a loose knot. Her legs looked impossibly long in the court shoes she was wearing, which surprised her - she couldn't remember the last time she'd worn heels. And of course, she wasn't wearing her broken beetle-green glasses. Even a thin layer of scotch tape twirled around one arm was horribly visible when she'd tried them on, and so she'd been forced to wear some contacts that she'd found in the back of her bedside drawer at three o-clock that morning. She hoped they were all right. Did contacts go out of date? She blinked experimentally, and her reflection came into sharper focus. A smart woman in a suit stared firmly back at her as the elevator whispered down to the ground floor.

Fia knew she could belong here, if they gave her a chance to prove it. It didn't matter if those men didn't see it; she did. This reflection was professional to the core, and so could she be. She understood everything in the envelope Louella had given her; it was all easy to grasp. She could follow all the arguments in the documents well. They weren't better than her; they were just on home ground. Her expression tightened, and the tears that threatened to fall just misted her contacts for a moment.

Maybe there was no mystery to it; maybe it wasn't any wonder that horrible man hadn't recognised her. She barely recognised herself. She let her fingertips just touch the cold metallic reflection of her face. What was it that Louella had said the week before, when they were sitting on her living room carpet, drinking tea? 'Learn to appreciate yourself, and then it doesn't matter if other people don't' - this was a good moment to put that into practice. She took a red permanent marker from her pocket, and drew a heart shape just beneath the reflection of her eye on the doors of the elevator. She hoped that they tried to clean it away, and couldn't.

"Never mind," she whispered to her reflection, as it blinked slowly back at her. "Tomorrow is another day."

The doors of the elevator opened, but the atrium was not the oasis of peace that Fia remembered on the way in. She could hear shouting and screaming before she'd even stepped through the orange trees and beeped through the turnstiles, and then she made out the quiet sound of Louella trying to talk over it, sounding quite harried. Fia hurried to the reception desk; if Louella was even a tiny bit perturbed, there must be a big problem. Fia had only seen her upset twice in her entire life.

When she rounded the corner, she saw a

woman screaming every swear-word in the dictionary, her face turning purple with rage as she threatened the staff and their entire families, listing all the terrible fates that she hoped would befall them. As Louella tried and failed to calm her down, she tore the reception phone from its cradle and threw it onto the floor, where it shattered. She swept the potted plants and leaflets from one end of the counter to the other, and then tried to actually climb over the desk itself to claw at Louella, who smartly took some steps backwards away from her.

Security arrived a moment later, but they had barely managed to get a grip on the woman when she caught hold of a heavy bundle of official documents and threw them into Louella's face.

Fia wondered later that night whether she was always destined to be irrationally angry after talking to that damn lawyer with the Mercedes. This high level of frustration was still burning through her bloodstream when she saw her best friend flinch backwards, trying to protect herself from a flurry of papercuts. Confidential files flew either side of the counter, and she could see Louella frantically collecting as much as many of them back together as she could, but she couldn't reach the pages that fountained down the front of the desk.

"Damn it," said Fia, and began to run towards the mayhem.

The angry client stamped her feet, and began to grind the paperwork into the tiles. She was still screaming, and Fia could now make out some of her full sentences.

"Fakes, liars," her voice echoed from the polished walls. "How could I lose the case? Why did your lawyers represent my husband? Why?"

She stamped her foot down again, square in the centre of a loose page, and tore through it with her heel. It slipped on the tiles, and the woman's feet went out from under her. She went straight down onto the floor, catching her head on the edge of the reception desk as she fell. Blood dripped down the countertop, and splattered onto the floor.

The security guards tried to restrain her, but Fia was there by then. She put one hand on the woman's shoulder as she knelt beside her, using most of her slight body weight to hold her down.

"She needs the first aid kit," said Fia firmly. "Please can someone fetch it for me?"

"Tony," said Louella, pointing at one of the guards who stood beside her.

The man who must be Tony nodded, and went to find it as the woman tried to struggle to stand once more.

"Oh no you don't," Fia said firmly, pouring all of her annoyance into the words. "If you get up from this floor, I will have to go to all the effort of putting you back down on it, and that's a waste of time for both of us."

But the woman didn't listen, and she continued to try and push herself upwards. As she managed to get some weight on her feet Fia sighed, and deftly swept them back out from under her with one hook of her arm.

Louella just snorted, her arms full of dog-eared papers. "Please don't move, Madam," she said. "Head injuries are no laughing matter, after all. You might have a concussion."

Fia took the first aid kit from the security guard and opened it, placing its contents in a line on the desk. When she looked down, she was grateful to see that the woman had taken the easy option and was still sitting on the floor, legs stretched out over the bundle of paperwork and blood streaming from her forehead. Fia took out a roll of gauze and some disinfectant, and applied pressure to it.

"Don't worry, I can fix this," she said. "My mother was a paramedic, and she made sure I could bandage a wound before I was ten. But you'd better be polite while I do it, or you might get one over your mouth as well. Do we understand each other?"

"And you'd better not be bleeding on the paperwork," Louella hissed, snatching it free from beneath her legs, "Or I'm going to be quite ticked off."

Fia smiled. They had always worked well together, her and Lou. After all the teenage years of mischief they'd spent together, they had each other's back without even needing to open their mouths and ask, and it was impossible not to have complete trust in someone when you knew every mistake they'd made since they were still flat-chested and believed in Santa. It was such a shame she wouldn't get the job, but there was nothing to be done about that now. She sealed the end of the bandage and helped the troublemaker to her feet.

"All done. I'll leave you in the hands of these two gentlemen. You might need an ambulance – no? Are you sure?"

The woman was shaking her head now; her embarrassment was obviously kicking in.

"Then I'll leave you. Are you okay, Lou?"

"Of course. I'll speak to you later."

"Then goodbye."

And with that, Fia walked out of the high-rise and left the car crash of an interview behind her.

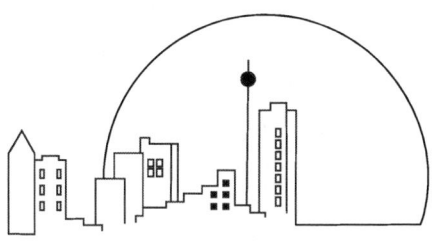

CHAPTER FOUR

Fia stepped inside her tiny flat, and closed the old, chipped front door behind her. She ran to the dipped cushions of her old sofa as soon as she managed to kick off her shoes, sinking into them and curling up in their familiar comfort. She lay there for what seemed like an eternity, breathing in the smell of her favourite camellia room scent, and began to wonder when she'd become such an embarrassing burden on people.

She hadn't even wanted to go to that interview in the first place. She knew how pitiable Louella must have found her to even recommend her for the post; she wouldn't risk her job otherwise. It was getting ridiculous now.

There was a time when Fia was happy with

her own career, although it was becoming a dimmer memory every time her alarm clock woke her up in the morning. This time last year, she was becoming more well-known with every passing month; there was even a time when she'd been interviewed on a podcast that had done well on social media. Although the experience had terrified her at the time, she now found herself wishing she was doing another one, just to prove she was good at something.

That man might sit there comfortably in his high-rise office, laughing at her for her 'little stories' but she was a good children's author. She had the reviews to prove it, and she reminded Louella about that on the phone later that evening, when she called to see how the interview had panned out.

"It... went," said Fia.

"Don't take it to heart, sweet pea," Louella soothed. "I know how successful you should be. That crappy illustrator can't hold out forever. You'll get your book back in no time."

Fia picked up the photo frame that stood on the table next to her sofa. Her brother Paul smiled out at her, his arm around picture-Fia's shoulder, both of them trapped behind the glass. Picture-Fia looked happy, and the future for her had been bright.

They'd been the perfect team. She'd always written the words and Paul had drawn the illustrations for her, right up to the day that she'd lost him. He was still drawing for her in his hospital bed, cursing when the cannula in his hands made them shake and he coloured outside of the lines.

He'd only stopped working on their last book to create her a goodbye-present, bullying the nurses into turning a blind eye to the canvas that he'd propped against the hospice wall, and the splashes of dried gouache that almost turned the floor into a painting itself. The book had remained unfinished, but Fia didn't have the heart to hate him for it, not when she saw the painting that he'd made for her.

Paul had saved his most beautiful artwork for last. It was the evening star, surrounded by sunset clouds and baby dragons. She didn't have the courage to hang it on the wall and look at it; she couldn't cry every day. The sensible part of her also knew it would never fit in her tiny apartment – the picture would take up the entire space of her wall. Paul always thought bigger than she did.

It was always going to be impossible to replace her brother's personal touch with her books, but her editor had been firm about it - and the attempt had gone more badly than she could have imagined. Maybe she could have been more friendly to the new illustrator that her agent had found for her, but discussing artwork reminded her too much of Paul, and she spent too much time disagreeing with him. Then he had turned on her. An email arrived, demanding author rights, claiming input into her manuscript that never took place. Threatening a lawsuit without credit, and a lot more royalties. The book was buried, and Fia hadn't opened a word document since.

"There should be something we can do. Even if you don't get the job, maybe I could ask one of the lawyers to look at the contract for you. We could find a way to force him to release the copyright-"

"No." Louella fell silent on the other end of the phone, and Fia sighed. "I appreciate it. You've done enough to help, and I'm grateful. No more."

She'd start looking for another job tomorrow morning, and that was all there was to it.

Later, Fia drowned the crawling sensation on her skin in a bubble bath, her long hair floating around her and the bubbles tickling her knees. She grew pink from the heat of it. She imagined the second-hand embarrassment of the day leaving her body and leaking into the hot water as she sank her head below the waterline. The bubbles crackled around her ears and she let her mind wander, and she suddenly thought of a pair of grey eyes, and an amused expression that lit them up.

He was beautiful, she realised. Damn him for that; for his long fingers that wrapped around his coffee cup, and the square shoulders inside his suit.

He'd popped the button free on his jacket with just one hand when he sat down. She wondered how broad his shoulders would be underneath it; what it would be like to run her hands up inside the jacket lining and feel them for herself in the tight space beneath the expensive fabric. She'd take care not to pull at his tight white shirt with the two buttons undone at the neck. It would expose his throat more, and she'd probably lick it. She'd have to sit on his lap to do it.

She pressed her legs tight together, and felt a pressure at the top of them. Yes, he was beautiful, and it was such a shame. Good looks were always wasted on bastards like that. She let one of her hands wander down her body through the hot water and run through her wet curls there. He was an expensive idiot, the worst kind. And he seemed to fluster easily for a calm lawyer. Why did she like it when he was flustered?

She pushed one finger between her legs and crooked it towards her. It was enough to make her draw breath immediately. Her hips rocked, and water splashed over the edges of the bath. She couldn't remember the last time she'd thought about someone when she did this. He was a terrible person, rude, with sparkling eyes. She liked it when he ran out of words. When she parted herself, the water scalded her - but she liked the heat, and she pressed her fingers in.

Twenty minutes later she was wrapped in a fluffy towel, pouring herself a glass of wine from the fridge and determined never to think about him again. Half an hour later, she caught herself thinking about the way he frowned at her, and in a last-ditch effort at sanity she drew an imaginary box in her brain, and sunk him into it.

Thank God she never had to see the idiot again in real life- it was lucky that the company hadn't taken her application seriously. It would have been hell to be stuck in a building with him day after day.

Of course, at that moment her phone rang. She didn't recognise the number, but she pressed the green icon and held it to her ear. After a polite "Who is this?" the voice on the other end identified himself as Darby. He offered her the position, starting the following Monday. Her behaviour at the desk had been very impressive, he said.

"A strong personality like yours will be an asset to us," he explained. "A firm hand, right? You knew exactly how to handle her. Very smart, and cool-headed. She threatened to sue, of course, but that's a silly threat to make in a building full of lawyers. I'm not concerned. Welcome to the team, we'll see you on Monday morning."

"Of course," managed Fia, and the line went dead. She took a long drink from the wine glass and topped it up from the fridge immediately. Oh well. Louella would be over the moon that her plan had worked, and at least Fia's own financial worries would be gone. She would go to bed, and text her once she was under the blankets.

Two glasses of wine later she was still there, slowly dripping water onto the kitchen floor.

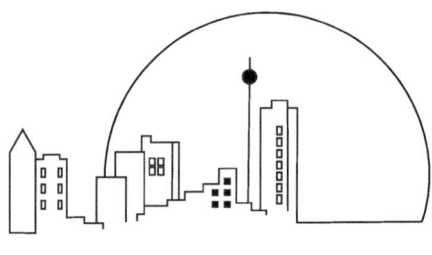

CHAPTER FIVE

Two things were guaranteed to happen every time that the main doors opened. Firstly, a blast of hot air would signal the arrival of another subdued visitor, and secondly Fia would have to shake the fog of boredom from her brain and act as though she was awake.

She'd already counted all the oranges on the trees.

"This is dull," she grumbled as another client made their way to the correct floor.

"It won't always be," reassured Louella, who was updating the meeting schedule on the screen they shared. "You'll be swamped with extra paperwork as soon as I've shown you how to do it. Consider today an early birthday present."

"All these people are so quiet when they come in."

"Yes, well." Louella clicked the mouse mischievously at her. "They have secrets to keep. You don't usually make that much money by behaving well."

"It's a shame." Fia tried to calculate the cost of the decorations in the entrance way and gave up. "If vulnerable people had a chance to use this support, we could fix a lot of problems. I mean, do you ever wonder if these people even deserve so much help?"

Her friend shook her head decisively. "No, I don't. Live and let live, that's my motto. I've got no right to comment on their life. I expect some of these people would frown on my behaviour, and I'm not going to do the same thing to them."

A pop-up message appeared on the screen in front of them and Louella swore under her breath. "I have to take something to a meeting in the main boardroom – Darby won't wait. Keep an ear out for the telephone while I'm gone. And you'd be surprised, Fia. We do some great outreach work here - just wait until you hear about some of it. Even your little activist-heart will melt a bit, I promise."

Another pop-up. This one wasn't as polite. Louella shrugged apologetically, and pulled some files from a cabinet behind her. "If you need me, come and find me," she called as she hurried off.

Fia was left alone. She listened to the quiet hum of conversation between the security guards and risked giving them a small wave, her shoulders relaxing when they returned it. She rolled them experimentally. It had been a while since she'd had to stand up for so long, and her back was beginning to burn. She crossed her arms behind her and stretched, pushing her shoulder blades backwards and feeling her spine pop. Her new silk shirt buttons pulled tight across her chest, but the feeling was so good.

The door hushed open, and she looked up. It was that grumpy lawyer again. Of course it is, she told herself. He works here, so he'll be walking through reception at least twice a day. Great. He seemed to be looking at her with an arrested expression on his face. She looked down, and saw that the fine silk of her blouse had pulled tightly around her breasts, hugging their entire outline. Oh no. She relaxed her shoulders and smiled apologetically. The fabric pooled back into its innocent folds, and outraged eyes made their way to her face.

"Some professionalism, please," he said.

"I'm sorry. My back was hurting."

"Then wear flat shoes, or a bigger shirt. I don't care what you come to work in, as long as you are professional. Just, don't do that. Ever again."

"I'm sorry..." but what was his name? Fia

couldn't remember the introduction; she'd been too worried about him recognising her. Still, the judgemental look on his face was extremely familiar, and so she refused to feel too badly about it. She doubted that he remembered hers, after all.

"I'm sorry Sir," she said eventually, when she'd finished searching her brain and come up empty.

His eyes widened. "Are you playing games with me?" he asked.

"No, Sir." She really wasn't. "I'm here to help. What can I do for you?"

"Open the gates for me, please. I've left my identity card in my office. I have a few errands that need running, but I'll wait until your co-worker returns; it needs someone competent. Send me a message when she's back."

"Of course, Sir."

Was it her imagination, or did he jump slightly when she called him that? Interesting. She liked the idea that she could disrupt his day a little; it was a little payback after the hurdles he'd put in her way recently. She pressed the release button for the gate, and he walked away in the direction of the orange trees.

The next woman to walk through the doors stood out from the others that had arrived that day,

43

because a small shape walked next to her, tripping along in her shadow. This was the first time Fia had seen a child in the place. The little boy clutched his mother's handbag tightly and tried to swing on it, dragging his feet along the polished floor and making his shoes squeak.

"How can I help you?" Fia asked.

The boy jumped when he heard her voice, and she smiled. Of course, he was too short to see her over the desk, and he didn't know she was there. She waved a peppermint candy at him from the bowl in front of her, and after a short nod from his parent he stuck it in his mouth.

The mother just pulled out a handful of papers from her handbag and slapped them onto the front desk. "Custody arrangements, for the divorce," she said.

Fia froze, and looked at the boy, now crunching away happily. She wanted to cover up his little ears, but he seemed deaf to his mother's words. "Do you want me to arrange a meeting for you to discuss your... issues? Just let me know the name of your solicitor and I'll find you a comfortable seat. Maybe your son-"

"Darby Bard," the mother interrupted. "He'll want this information as soon as possible. I don't understand why you're still standing there - just take it to him at once. He's one of your founding partners, isn't he, Darby? He should have my husband's position statement already. You'd better not keep me waiting at this damn draughty desk for long."

"He's representing both of you?"

"Yes. It will be quicker. He's a family friend."

Fia tried to remember all the legal information that had been thrown at her during her first week, and her brow furrowed. "Are you sure you can do that?"

"I can see you're new. Don't worry, I know exactly what I'm doing, and that paperwork explains my position very clearly. Pass it on, I haven't got all day." The client ignored Fia's attempted reply, and rummaged around in her bag once more, dropping a packet of rice cakes at her feet. "That will feed you for a while, darling," she said, and then she shoved the papers forward on the desk. By the time Fia had gathered the sheaf together again there was no sign of either the woman or the little boy in the entranceway.

This was very odd. Darby Bard only had one meeting set up for today, and this was the one Louella had gone to take the evidence to. It must be very important, because he'd cleared his entire day, and the messages he'd sent them about it were very short and to the point. They weren't his usual carefree style, that was for sure. Was this a scam? The scams in the City were getting worse if they'd started to involve little children now.

Without reaching a clear answer herself, Fia

decided a little more experience was needed, and so she went to find Louella in the office.

"What is it?"

"Someone left this information here. She says it's for Darby, but I can't see any record of a client meeting set up for him today. Do I give it to her?"

"Let me look." Louella took the papers and flicked through them. She hummed, and opened the file she had with her. "This is the paperwork I took upstairs for his meeting earlier. The surnames match."

"She said Darby was representing both of them," said Fia, but her friend shook her head at this.

"No, he can't be. That's not legal. This is a mix-up; we'll have to inform Darby, then call the woman and let her know we can't represent her. This isn't going to be my favourite case though."

Louella showed Fia the two position statements. Both parents were refusing custody.

"Neither of them want that little boy?" she felt sick. "You mean, they're arguing to get rid of him?"

No matter how much she didn't want to believe it, it must be true, because there it was, written down in black ink on solid white paper. Both of the parents wanted to relinquish one hundred per cent of care and child support. Fia must have had a dark expression on her face, because her friend gently tapped her on the shoulder.

"Don't worry, babes. This won't fly with Darby for one short minute. He's a great believer in family. He has two little girls himself; he just worships them - you just wait until you're alone with him and he runs you through all the pictures of them that he has on his phone."

Fia smiled. At least there were some good ones in the world. "Are we supposed to be reading all of these case notes?" she asked.

"Louella was suddenly a dark cloud of offended affront. "Well, we didn't even know these were official case notes until I checked, did we? And we'll be fine as long as no one finds out."

There was a knock on the office door. Both women jumped, and Louella hid the files behind her back in one smooth movement. It cracked open a little, and one of the security guards peeped through.

"Lou?"

"Yes, Tony, what is it?"

Tony pushed the door open all of the way and shuffled slowly into the room. Fia gasped when he saw the bundle he clasped in his wide arms - it was the little boy himself, all curly hair and elbows and knees.

"I found this leaving sticky hand prints on the windows. It says it's hungry. No-" he was distracted for a moment, "No little fella, you can't play with Uncle Tony's taser. Let go. And stop wriggling around like the inside of a washing machine. Have some manners, yeah?"

The tiny child seemed to concentrate at that. "Manners," he said. He sucked his thumb.

"Yeah kid, manners. Well done." Tony seemed exhausted as he looked to the women. "Has anyone lost a child?" he asked.

The mother had left without him. She'd thrown him a snack, and run away from him as if he was an unwanted kitten.

Fia didn't think it could get any worse, but as she flicked back through the paperwork the woman had given her at the desk, she revealed another problem.

"We'll have to call Darby now," she said as Tony jiggled his yawning passenger. "There's no contact information on the statements at all – not on a single page. We can't get back in touch with the mother – she's made sure of it."

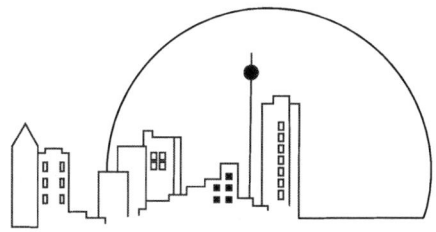

CHAPTER SIX

But it wasn't Darby that came running down the stairs, and pushed through the emergency exit sign to meet them in the lobby - it was the stern lawyer that disapproved of Fia. She wondered how on earth she could be so unlucky.

"What's this about a child?" he asked shortly, as he drew closer to them.

"Here, sir," said Tony, offering up the young boy in his arms. "I've got him. But I really should get back to the doors; they're unmanned. Can someone take him from me?"

The lawyer just frowned, and backed away from the infant. "If you're not on the doors, then who's at reception?" he asked.

Louella and Fia both hesitated. Louella made

49

her move first, and headed back towards the desk. Tony just stood there rigid, and in the end Fia stepped forward and took the little boy into her arms as he almost ran back to his position at the main doors.

"Could Darby not make it?" she asked.

"He's in a meeting. I was closer. What happened?"

Fia explained, and his mouth set in a firmer and firmer line as she continued talking.

"So - you're trying to tell me," he interrupted, "That you paid such little attention to reception that someone was able to *abandon a child,* and you didn't notice for twenty minutes?"

Fia stopped explaining. The boy began to shift in his sleep, and it took all she had to keep a grip on him. "Yes, Sir," she said in defeat.

"I can't believe Darby hired you. He's too soft-hearted for his own good."

The child moved again, and tried to turn over. He slipped between Fia's elbows, and she wondered if she could lower the dead weight of him gently to the floor, before her arms gave way entirely. The lawyer sighed in frustration and took him out of her arms. He held the boy with a gentle awkwardness, as though he was cradling a bomb that might go off at any moment. Fia was pretty sure he'd never held a child before.

"Am I that bad?"

Fia turned to see Darby Bard himself. He'd finally managed to extricate himself from his meeting and join them, and his brow furrowed with concern when he saw the young child in Joel Bard's firm grip.

"You are, and you know it. And now you're finally here, do you want to take the boy? You've got far more experience in this than I have." The boy in question was now slipping in his arms; his legs were now wrapped around the lawyer's knees.

"Um, no thank you - you can keep him. He's got nothing to do with me, after all. Think of it as practice," Darby replied swiftly. "One day you might be able to persuade someone to have a child with you, as unlikely as it may seem. I'll let you improve yourself."

"Fine." He hauled the child upwards and resettled him, one sleepy cheek resting on his shoulder.

The boy's heels un-tucked his shirt as they rose, and Fia could see an inch of tanned skin flexing above his waistband. She blinked. Were those freckles? The news report she'd listened to this morning had said that this was the longest summer for years, and almost everybody had a deeper suntan than ever before, but where on earth had this man been topless? He didn't seem the type; he was all starched shirts and ties. She caught herself, she'd been staring for too long, and he'd seen her. He pulled the white linen back down with a firm tug and turned away.

"This is a terrible situation," said Darby, compelled to fill in the silence. "Thank you for helping, Fia."

"Helping?" Joel Bard was incredulous. "She *caused* this entire mess. We can hire someone better, Darby. Anyone. The office cleaner would do a better job. I'm not comfortable keeping her on-"

"Can't your concerns wait until we've decided what to do with the child?"

The lawyer sighed. "Fine." He spared one final glance at Fia. "Get back to work, and try and do better."

She took the hint, and began to make a retreat to the reception desk, but she wasn't more than three steps away before he began to talk about her again. As she reached the orange trees she made a split decision to listen to him, and so she tucked herself behind the slim trunk of the nearest one with barely a rustle to the polished leaves on the spreading branches above her.

"She's a liability."

She heard the anger in his voice, the dark gravel of it.

"I want her here. What on earth do you have against the woman? If she's making you uncomfortable you could at least tell me why," retorted Darby.

Fia strained to hear the reply, waiting to hear what the reason was. It had been years since she'd held down a proper job, and being a self-employed writer meant a lot of time alone. Maybe her social skills were failing her – maybe she'd said something wrong, maybe she'd been interacting badly with the clients.

Of course, he could remember her from the car park, in which case it was entirely his fault and she refused to feel guilty about it. But-

"No reason, she's just extremely unprofessional," was the only answer.

"She'll learn. Louella is a good teacher. Just leave her be, will you? I've made my decision, and you know I never ask you for much. I promised she could have a decent try at it."

"Dear God, why?"

"This really seems to be upsetting you, doesn't it? I've never known you have such a strong reaction to any member of staff. Usually, you don't even notice them - you can't even remember their names."

"I don't know her name," came the grudging answer. "But I suppose she's the least of our worries at the moment. What are we going to do with the child?"

"Just call social services, it's all we can do," said Darby with a sad sigh. "He's just got to get out of

the building at this point. This place isn't suitable for a child at all."

"No. I won't agree to that just yet." The anger in the voice grew darker still. "This poor boy is completely innocent in the mess that his parents have created, after all. Let's just make sure he's all right, Darby, since we've found him. We'll keep him with us at the moment, just until his mother wants him back. I'm sure it won't be long until she misses him."

"Why are you making this sound personal?"

"I'm not, for God's sake. I just want to make sure that the kid is all right."

"If you insist."

"I absolutely do."

Darby laughed. Fia heard the elevator doors open, and soon they were gone. She tried to stop worrying about the little boy, and found it easier than she expected, knowing that he was in the arms of that lawyer. She might not trust that man with many things, but strangely, she believed he meant it when he said he would care for the child.

It was safe to leave the orange tree, but she stayed where she was for a moment and rested her forehead against the rough bark of its slim trunk. Why was she so pissed off? She wasn't offended that he didn't know her name; she didn't know his after all – but his opinion of her made her heart hurt.

Maybe it was because his was the second time

in her life that she'd been called unprofessional, and it stung just as sharply the second time around. Maybe it was because both times were so unjust. Paul's replacement, the illustrator her editor had hired, had called her the same thing. He'd said she should learn to share - he'd told everyone in the industry that Fia couldn't work well with others. It didn't matter to anyone that he was the thief; that he was trying to steal her brother's last book; many of them believed him.

She pulled at a tiny leaf from the tree, barely uncurled and ready to grow, full of potential with just one little job to do. When did everything get so complicated for humans?

If only she could hide in her tiny apartment, and order food to be delivered every day as she wrote her stories, far away from other people. If only she could open her laptop, or pick up a pen. Until then she was stuck at this place.

She sighed, and straightened up, rubbing at her forehead and hoping that she didn't have an impression of the bark imprinted onto it. This moping around did no good. Tomorrow was a new day, and she would do better, and so Fia started walking back to the front desk to act like the professional receptionist that she needed to be. She'd be damned if he was going to be right about her.

Louella threw an arm around her for a brief moment as they stood together at the reception desk, and Fia stood there in the little warm bubble of welcome that she projected.

"Never mind," her friend said. "Ignore them."

"They think I'm stupid," replied Fia morosely.

"Then they don't know you at all. I've known you since you were six, and I know you aren't stupid. Listen to me, not them."

"I've never felt so useless!"

"You're just a little out of your depth. You'll start to swim soon; I just know it." Louella's shoulders began to shake, and Fia bumped her hard with her hip.

"Shut up, and stop laughing at me – I know you're enjoying this." Then she gestured to all the paraphernalia on the desk; the diaries, the screens and the payment machines. "I've had enough of being the weakest link around here; it's time that I learned something. How does all this work?"

"Are you serious?"

"Show me." Fia picked up a tablet with a list of questions at it, and poked at it with the attached stylus. It made no sense to her at all. "I'll learn it all this afternoon. I mean, how hard could it be?"

Louella stepped back, and took in the implacable look on Fia's face. "All right, I'll help you - but it's going to take more than a day, Fia. Don't put yourself under that much pressure, for goodness' sake

- you'll show them who you are soon enough. And I'll introduce you to someone who can help; a man called James. He's Darby's assistant; no one understands the systems around here more than he does. If he likes you, he can upgrade your clearance so you can help with the cases."

"Like you?"

"Yes, like me. Now, hand me that pen. I'll write you a list."

Fia did as she was told.

A few days later, Louella paused a telephone call, and pointed out James as he walked towards the turnstiles in reception. Fia realised at once that he was someone that she'd often seen around the building, but had never had the chance to meet. He was a thin, nervous-looking man who always wore his pinstripe suits a little long, and as a result they puddled into little folds around his ankles. Maybe he thought it made his legs look less lanky, but in reality he just looked like he was hiding little springs beneath his clothes. Fia wondered how high he could jump.

"That's him." Louella dug an elbow into Fia's side as she gestured in his direction. "I'll call him over to talk to you."

"Will he mind?"

"Not at all – he'll be annoyingly happy about the whole thing. Don't be put off with how self-important he is; that man can be very useful; that's why he gets away with his attitude. He'll love telling you how essential his work is - but just be aware that once he *starts* talking, it might be a bit difficult for him to stop."

"But I don't have that long," Fia hissed. "You know my agent's making me go to that book event. She says it's the least I can do, when I haven't written anything in over a year. I have to walk out of this building right on time today -"

"- James!" Louella called, "Come and meet Fia, she's been dying to meet you."

The man hesitated by the turnstile, his identity badge held delicately between two fingers. He tucked it away inside his shirt once he recognised Louella, and came to meet them.

"Good afternoon, ladies," he said generously. "How goes your day?"

"Spiffing," said Louella, but he didn't seem to hear the joke at his expense. "You arrived at just the right moment. Fia here was interested in the protocols we work with, and I thought, well, who understands them better than James? Do you think you could have a little conversation with her? Are you in that much of a rush?"

"*I* am," whispered Fia rebelliously, but she just received another dig in the ribs for her trouble.

James' eyes brightened immediately. He

shuffled behind the reception desk, squeaked over a wheeled office chair and sat slightly too close to Fia. Soon she was being bombarded by deadlines, court email addresses, the names of useful clerks and the best coffee shops in the area to visit during her lunch break.

"Thank you, James," said Fia, and found she meant it. "Louella told me that you're Darby's assistant, but it seems as though you're much more than that – you do so much!"

James nodded solemnly; to him a truer word had never been spoken. His limp hair fell into his eyes, and he brushed it away with a flourish. "Hmm, I suppose it does look that way. The partners are always so busy around here; they need all the help they can get. I've been Darby Bard's secretary for seven years – ever since he began to take on the more complicated cases, and I suppose I've learned it all with him. I barely notice the workload now."

"I'm glad I'm just the second receptionist," she said with feeling.

"Don't worry," he said to her, patting her hand encouragingly. It was a classic move to check for a wedding ring, and Fia pulled away from him at once. "Once you're more used to it here then you'll fit right in. I think it's incredibly brave to tackle this role, with no previous experience. Darby was just mentioning it the other day, when we were listing all the awards the company is nominated for this year. He's very proud of you."

"Award nominations? That sounds impressive."

"It is, but just think – soon you'll be a part of it all too, won't that be wonderful?"

Fia glanced at her watch and winced slightly when she realised how late it was. If she was any longer getting out of the building, then she'd miss her train and her agent would wash her hands of her completely.

"Yes, I can't wait to do more for the company, I promise," she cut him off before he could get into his stride again, "But right now I have a meeting to get to, and it'll take me a while to travel there. Maybe I could speak to you about this another day?" She named the bookshop; it was on the opposite side of the City.

"Of course! I'll take your mobile number - we can arrange another time." James seemed far too happy about getting her contact details, and Fia watched him tap the numbers into his phone with a wince. "But let me take you there? It's dangerous for a woman to travel alone, and it's already growing dark outside." He waved away her growing reluctance with something that almost passed for charm. "I insist on coming with you."

Fia didn't have time to put him off, and so she

agreed reluctantly; as she clocked out she saw Tony rolling his eyes at her, but she managed to walk to the station on schedule.

They took the sky train together across the City. James was surprisingly silent during the trip; he didn't start any conversations at all, and when she asked him a question about his lunch hours he just muttered the word 'confidentiality' in a knowing way, and spent most of the time gazing at the buildings out of the window. Fia sat next to him and did the same, watching the neon lights winking from the sides of the canyon cliffs in the rapidly-darkening sky. She began to wonder just how often he actually left the offices. It seemed like everyone in that place was a terrible workaholic.

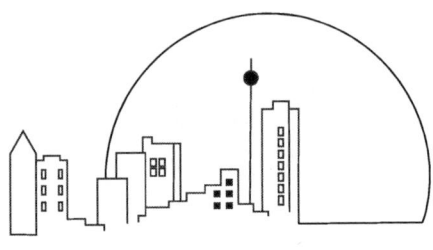

CHAPTER SEVEN

The smell of paper and ink hit Fia smartly in the face the moment she opened the door of the bookshop, and the familiarity of it stung. She almost turned around and went straight back home, but she could see her agent waiting for her in the corner of the shop floor. Besides, even if she was brave enough to disappear in plain sight of the woman, James was now in the doorway behind her. She had no other options but to continue now her escape route was blocked, and so she stepped inside and breathed deeply until her nausea began to fade.

James seemed more out of his depth than she did, and that helped her recover. He was lost in a sea of publishing executives, online bloggers and reviewers from social media. The low hum of conversation all centred around the new book release her agent was promoting, and they all clasped a copy of it in their arms. Fia watched him hovering, and took pity on him.

"The romance section," she said.

"Oh no, that's not my style," said James at once. "I haven't had a chance to read a book in years, I'm kept so busy, but my tastes always used to run to action-adventure. Mummies, ghosts, that sort of thing – like all boys before they go to university, I suppose."

"And spies," said Fia thoughtfully. "But that's not what I mean. Go and read through some of the romance novels; it'll help you to get a date."

He bristled. "I don't need an instruction manual, Fia. I'm more than capable of talking to women once they've noticed me, and I assure you -"

"I don't mean that," she reassured him. "Look, go to the romance section - pick up several books and put them back down again, while looking very lost and confused. When one of the women there comes over to ask you if you need any help, tell her you're not sure about trying a new genre, but that you're looking for anything with a happy ending."

Really? Will that work?"

"Like a charm. They're all a bunch of hopeless romantics over there. You'll be rescued by a lady in shining armour, and then you can offer to take her out to coffee as a thank you. Now," Fia could see her agent bearing down on her, "Off you go, and I wish you well, I don't know any man that deserves a date more than you do; any woman would be lucky!"

James took no more convincing. He straightened his shoulders, and headed straight for a collection of bright pink novellas, shuffling through them with realistic confusion painted onto his face. Fia turned to her agent, and tried to remember that novel writing was her proper day job, and not the legal firm that seemed to be taking over her life at the moment.

"Well, Fia, long time no see," she said. "Let's go and help with the promotion, shall we?"

Fia nodded, watching her colleague out of the corner of her eye. He was already deep in conversation with a short brunette with a kind face, who was suddenly tugging at his sleeve and pulling him in the direction of the historical romance section. It seemed like her plan was working, and she was happy she could help James a little bit in return; he was doing so much for her.

This lucky introduction soon melted the thin defences of Darby's assistant, and so several days later Fia found herself at an Italian restaurant, absent-mindedly picking at the wax drips that wound their way around an old bottle with a candle stuck in it. James was more than thirty minutes into a description of the wonderful nature of his new girlfriend, and she hadn't even had a chance to glance at the wine list.

"Choose whatever you'd like," he said, gesturing at the menu. "It's on me. I'd never have thought of a bookshop as a place to meet someone; you really do have a keen mind, Fia. I'm incredibly grateful."

"I'm glad you think so," Fia replied with a laugh. "You're the first person at work to compliment me; I'm afraid my reputation there isn't so good. Louella says I just need to give it some time, but I'm not so sure. Anyway, I'm glad I was useful this once. I'll just have to use any opportunity I can to prove it at the office."

"Well..." James thought for a moment, and then a kind smile crossed his face. "I could bump you up a level of clearance. Then you'd be able to help Louella more efficiently; it would level the playing field a bit."

Fia blinked at him in the dim light of the restaurant. "Can you do that?"

"Honestly? I've already got Darby to agree to it. He was in a very good mood this morning, and so I thought of you and seized the moment. Just think of it as a thank you - I've been single for far too long." He laid a consent form down onto the chequered tablecloth, and waved a gilt- covered pen at her. "Just sign here, and I'll give you your new lanyard."

Fia stared at it, unable to believe her luck. "Thank you, I wasn't expecting -"

But she didn't know what else to say. She just signed the form at once, creating a pared-down version of her autograph, spending time making it look as presentable as possible. This was an important signature; her first step in proving what she was capable of. It deserved to look good, and so she added an extra swirl at the end, just for effect.

"Don't mention it," said James gravely, pocketing the paperwork and the pen. "I'm not sure I've done you a favour."

"What do you mean?"

"It's quite a workload. Be careful not to spend too many hours in the building, like the rest of us do, Fia. You'll end up single forever, trust me."

Fia laughed. "Bring it on," she said.

Fia returned from the dinner several hours later, after she'd consumed enough pasta to put an Italian grandmother into a two-day food coma. She also had a shiny new identity badge that could access all the areas that a lowly receptionist could ever hope to get into, and a deeper respect for the dark circles around the eyes of everyone that worked at JD Bard Associates.

Despite her full stomach, and the fact that her official working day had ended hours ago, Fia was determined to work late into the evening. She planned to figure out the layout of the filing system, so she could start on her new workload bright and early the following morning. The amount of food she'd eaten had severely slowed her down, and she was now very proud of herself for refusing dessert, and staying strong whenever James had tried to press it on her. The only issue was the sheer amount of garlic that had been in the pasta; it felt as though she was breathing it over everything as she walked.

In an effort to stay professional she rummaged in her handbag and took out a packet of chewing gum, removing a stick of it and popping it in her mouth as she approached the filing room - but she hesitated in the doorway when she heard someone rifling through papers inside it. She peered uncertainly through the door, just to see a square pair of shoulders inside a well-fitted jacket, and the familiar tousled dark hair that annoyed her so much.

"Come in, if you're going to come in, don't just hover and stare," he said.

Fia walked into the room, a little disappointed that the door was already open, and that she didn't get a chance to beep her new identity card on the door lock; it made her new shiny lanyard seem like a useless thing.

It was a little disappointing to find that the restricted area was just another glorified cupboard full of files that were yet to be digitised. Rows of ugly metal filing cabinets were shoved beneath overflowing shelves, and she inhaled a slight film of dust every time she took a breath. Fia scanned the bookshelves and began to tap the spines of the folders, muttering the names of the cases to herself. She could almost feel the disapproval radiating from the other side of the tiny room, but she was determined to ignore the man, even if they were almost bumping shoulders.

"Why are you here, poking around in areas above your paygrade? Are you spying?" he asked, eventually.

"I can look through the files," she replied defensively. "I've got the clearance now."

"Really?"

The look of genuine shock on his face began to needle her.

"There's no need to look so surprised," she said. "I work harder than you think I do, temporary position or not." She turned towards him as she spoke, but was unable to stare him down because her head only came up to his shoulder, and she suddenly felt awkward when she couldn't step far enough backwards in the space to see clearly into his face.

"Would you like me to leave you here, and come back later, Sir? I don't want to be in the way," she added quickly, suddenly feeling very unwelcome.

"I'm extremely unconcerned about any...

position that you happen to be in," he replied coolly. "Feel free to continue."

With this, he returned to his work, removing more files from the shelves and stacking them in several piles, or just taking one sheaf from them and placing the rest back exactly where he'd found them. It seemed very scientific. Fia tried to look busy, but this was difficult when she hadn't had a particular reason for being there in the first place.

"Don't you have an assistant to do that for you?" she asked shortly.

"I can fetch my own files, thank you very much. I'm more than capable."

Fia watched him work and she couldn't deny it; he turned the files over more quickly even than Louella did, not one iota of energy wasted. His efficiency irritated her beyond all reason.

"Don't worry; keep working hard and I'm sure you'll qualify for help soon. You're friends with the boss, so I expect that's helped you climb the ladder," she said. It sounded bitter, even to her ears.

"It's one way of getting on in life, I suppose," he said thoughtfully. "And here you are, newly-cleared for an assistant position. Are you suggesting yourself for the role? I wouldn't bother – just the thought of it horrifies me."

"Help you? I'd rather be unemployed and live in a tent," retorted Fia, the words coming out of her mouth before she'd had a chance to think about them.

He folded his arms in annoyance, and they brushed against her with the barest whisper. She was sure she could feel his warmth through the sleeves of his jacket. Fia inhaled sharply at the contact, and choked on her chewing gum.

The lawyer in front of her watched with wide eyes as it fell from her mouth and landed neatly on the floor in front of him, narrowly missing his sharp tailoring. It lay there, an offensive white splat on the floor, and Fia closed her eyes and refused to look at it.

"Do you really need to be told not to chew gum in here?" The frustration in his tone seemed to be coming from the direction of her knees. Fia opened her eyes to see him bending down, and removing a linen handkerchief from his pocket. He picked the gum up from the floor and stood again, seemingly unbothered that he was holding something that had once been in her mouth. "It's extremely unprofessional. What impression does that give - a receptionist chewing away like a cow in a field? Horrifying."

He threw the handkerchief neatly into the waste paper basket and dusted his fingertips. Fia tried not to think about how expensive it was.

"You use that word a lot; maybe you should

expand your vocabulary," she muttered. "No-one will see me anyway, it's too late for any clients to turn up – and at least I'm clean and fresh."

"What are you implying?"

"It's a small room, and you're breathing in front of me. Figure it out for yourself." Fia felt bad for saying it; the idea that this man was poorly-groomed was ridiculous.

"Easily fixed."

He smirked and reached for her hand, turning it over and tapping at her knuckles until she opened it. For a brief second he rested his warm palm against hers. She heard a rustle as his hand closed over the packet of gum that she was still holding, and he slid a stick of it free, gently unwrapping it from the bright foil.

"Do you mind?" he asked, folding it into his mouth.

He screwed up the empty packaging and slid it into the front pocket of her trousers, pushing it down firmly with two fingers until it was snugly nestled at the bottom of it, as far as it would go. The smell of mint filled the room as he bit down on the gum he'd taken, and then with a shrug he collected all the files he'd collated and left the room.

"Close the door behind you when you leave," he called back. "Make sure you hear the lock click."

"Damn it," said Fia when he'd gone, as she

rooted around in her pocket. "Why did he have to push it in so far?" She took another stick of gum, and defiantly chewed it as she returned to the reception desk, and the comfort of Louella.

"I'm not sure the increase in responsibility is going to be enough, Lou," she wailed, as her friend stroked at her hair and tutted. "It's going to take a miracle for me to fit in around here."

"Don't worry," her friend soothed. "You'll get there. You just need a project - something spectacular - something that will make them realise what an asset to the company you are. Just give it time, I'll keep my eye out for one for you."

"Thanks," said Fia, grimly. "I'll try not to muck it up."

Several days later she finally had her chance, and it came in the shape of Darby Bard, who looked extremely stressed. He was pulling at his curly hair so much that Fia was worried he'd take chunks of it out. His friendly smile was still there though; that would survive a nuclear apocalypse.

"Mr Bard," said Louella, standing forward at the desk. "How can I help you today?"

"Ah, you're going to regret that question," said Darby Bard, with a cheeky grimace beneath his smile. "I want to say this is about what I can do for you, but I think you'll see through me straight away. You're a smart lot down here on reception."

"I'm interested," said Louella, a smile in her voice.

"Well, as you know, and Fia here probably doesn't, we've won the Rose award again. I expect that has irritated the judges, because we are now hosting the event for it. I'd like to take this chance to invite you personally."

Fia thought that sounded like fun. "What did the company win the award for?" she asked.

"Well, that's an interesting question," said Darby with a smile. "Some pessimists say we bribe the judges, you know – but that's hardly fair. The world hasn't lost all its hope yet. No, it's my cousin. He insists on all this charity work in his spare time – environmental issues, wrongful arrests, that sort of thing."

"That's... commendable," said Fia, surprised.

"It is, I suppose. It doesn't bring any money into the company, so I have to rein him in a bit, but we do get this shiny trophy once a year. My cousin is part magpie, and I think this pleases him."

"Who's in charge of organising it?" asked Louella.

Darby just stared at her. Fia took the hint. This was their job, then. He smiled again as they both caught on.

"Good afternoon to you both, and I should

get going," he said. "You can expect the first arrangements next week."

"A party?" asked Fia as he left the building.

"Black tie. It always is. We'll be hosting representatives from every legal practice in the area. There will be caterers, decorators..." Louella fast-tapped a ballpoint pen on the computer monitor. "It's going to be a lot of work."

"I can run it for you, if you like," Fia offered.

Louella gave her an evaluating stare. "All right. Anything to save me from the hassle. Just make sure it's done well, for Heaven's sake."

"I will."

Fia looked forward to it. It was time to show the people that worked here what she was capable of; and by people, she meant one particular grumpy lawyer, although she'd deny that with her last breath, even in a court of law.

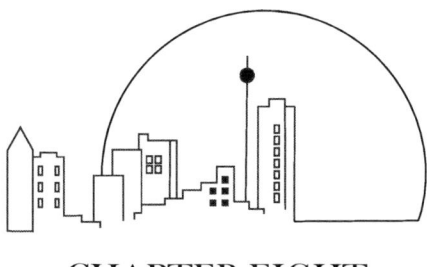

CHAPTER EIGHT

Storm season was approaching. The hot weather had boiled itself to an end, and thick clouds were beginning to gather in the skies. Everyone hoped that the rain would wait a few days, because Darby had chosen the rooftop of the high-rise as the main party venue.

"It will be fine," he'd said with a grin. "Trust me; I'm always right about this sort of thing."

The ground floor atrium had been converted into a stage for the main ceremony itself, and then the guests would retire to the fresh air high in the sky: either to dance and celebrate their victory, or to drown their losses at the bar. They just needed one more evening of sunshine, but security wasn't convinced that the rain would hold off.

"Cars will be arriving soon," said Tony, looking up at the clouds through the tinted windows and trying to work out how dark they were in real life. He adjusted his security uniform and went outside to check. He was such a huge man that even the largest size uniform didn't completely encase all of his muscles. Fia was worried that his shirt would split open the moment he got into any kind of serious fight.

She was working this evening, of course, but her outward appearance hid that fact, unlike Tony. Louella's new girlfriend had arrived at her house a few days ago and delivered a floor length gown in pearl grey, sewn over with sequins in sky blue. Ten minutes earlier, Louella herself had pressed a glass of white wine into her hand. She looked like a guest.

"You'd fool anyone in that," said Tony, walking back into the building. "You look like a mermaid; they'll never work out that you have a brain like a shark."

"Thank you, I think," said Fia with grace, taking a sip of her wine.

"It's damp."

"I beg your pardon?"

"The air out there. I think it might turn. If we had an umbrella down here, we could help people in from the cars if it starts coming down. Save them all looking like expensive drowned rats in the official pictures."

Fia remembered seeing some on the dance terrace. "I can fetch you one, Tony. Give me a few minutes."

Tony nodded once in thanks, and she headed for the roof.

The dance floor had been built over the past week; Fia had taken charge of the workmen herself. She made sure they only used the back entrance to the building, keeping the dust and wood shavings away from the pristine reception. It covered the entire roof, a glistening walnut floor decked with fairy lights and tiny orange lanterns that reminded her of the trees downstairs. The company certainly had a brand image.

She saw the stack of matching umbrellas on the far side, and took one. The wind ruffled it as she looked out over the city. It was going to be a beautiful party. Fia flicked a switch on the wall, and tiny freckles of light danced about her, reminding her of the stars that were hidden behind the clouds. A glitterball. The bright dots swam across her and the walls, and she smiled. It was like a school dance, or an old Hollywood movie. There was something old-fashioned and friendly about it. It wouldn't be like that in real life, though. The people downstairs would make their way through the party forming alliances and throwing friends under a bus. Tony was right, it was a shark tank, it was under the sea. She took a sip of her drink.

"What are you doing?"

She turned round. Of course, he was here.

"I'm on my way downstairs, Sir. I got lost."

The slight twitch, when she called him by that name. He brushed it off quickly before he replied to her.

"Then you can accompany me, can't you? God knows how many other interesting buttons you'll push if I leave you here alone. Leave the decorations to the catering staff."

Fia span slowly in a circle in the centre of the dance floor, humming a tune she remembered from the radio. She didn't know what magic was in the air up here, but she felt really good. "Shall we dance first?" she asked.

"I hate heights, so no. I'll stay by the door."

"I'll hold on to you, you'll be fine," she said, holding her arms in a waltz position. "We won't go near the edges."

A snort of disbelief, and a hand between her shoulder blades. "I don't have time. I'm giving the main speech downstairs in twenty minutes. You would know that, if you paid any attention to me at all."

"Fia shrugged. "I've got better things to do," she said.

"How nice for you. Now come on, it's time to leave." He turned the glitterball off, and walked towards the elevator. With no alternative, Fia followed him. She was still humming the tune when they entered it and the doors closed, but the atmosphere was so close in the small space that she soon stopped. He leaned against the back wall and closed his eyes.

"Are you okay?" she asked, wondering why she bothered. She didn't care – she didn't.

He huffed. "I'm remembering my speech. I'm fine. Pardon me if I concentrate for a moment."

"You're giving a speech?" Fia was surprised. It must be a progressive company that let one of their bank lawyers talk for them.

"Yes, obviously I am. I'm not sure what they'd do if I told them I wouldn't, honestly. Now, hush."

She shrugged, and left him to it. The elevator took a long time to descend from the rooftop space to the ground floor. He didn't say a word, but his cologne filled the space entirely. Fia breathed it in. Cinnamon warmed her lungs, and she felt a stab of frustration. It was one of her favourite scents. It reminded her of Christmas, and late breakfasts.

"I hope you didn't go to too much effort to write it. Everyone will just be waiting for you to finish so they can have a good time, you know," she said suddenly, unable to bear the silence any more. "Why don't you just thank them in the morning instead? Send an email."

For a moment she didn't think he'd said anything out loud, but then she heard "Better to get it over with," whispered under his breath.

"Sorry?" There was a slight grinding noise from the elevator, but she ignored it. "Wait, do you not like giving speeches? It's your job to talk in front of people, isn't it?"

"Well, I'm good at it. I never said I enjoyed it," he shot back at her. "Not all of us have signed up for a good party tonight, unfortunately. I hope you have a wonderful time."

His shoulders were very tense, now that she noticed them, and his harsh voice matched the screeching of the elevator as it came to a halt. The lights flickered, and he started in shock.

"Relax," Fia soothed, patting his chest gently. "I'll call for help."

He merely tutted, and pushed the alarm button on the wall. A call tone started to sound, but it didn't connect. They both listened to it quietly ring.

"I jumped because it was cold," he said.

Fia looked down at her half-empty wine glass. The jolt of the elevator had shaken it, and half of her wine was over his trousers.

"Sorry," she said in alarm, and reached down to pat there too. He caught her wrist to stop her.

"No," he said in a strangled voice. "I'd rather you not."

"Oh."

"We'll be out of here in a moment, I'm sure of it. Otherwise, I'll be hiring new maintenance staff. You don't need to be concerned."

"I don't think I'm as worried as you are," said Fia in a rare moment of honesty at work. "You look like a statue. You're terrified."

"Not about this situation, I promise."

"You're a bad actor, you know," she said, teasing him - anything to get that frozen look off his face. "What do you know about this elevator that I don't? Will it fall? Are we going to be stuck in here for hours?"

"No!" He seemed to battle with himself before giving in, and answering her question. "It's public speaking," he said, haltingly. "Everyone expects so much from me. I can't help feeling it's only a matter of time before I let them down."

Fia thought about that. "Will you?" she asked.

He smiled his fake, well-practiced smile. "Not today," he said. "And that's the important thing. I'm not concerned."

"You're as stiff as a board," she pointed out helpfully, mapping out his body height with one gesture from her wine glass. More spilt onto the floor. "Oh damn," she said, cursing her natural clumsiness.

It was proving far too difficult to pretend to be smooth at work.

She knelt on the floor, and tried to mop up some of the spillage just as he leaned forwards and jammed a finger against the call button again. Fia's cheek rested against his trousers for a brief unexpected minute, and she drew back to look at him. What was that? She stared at the front of him.

"You're hard," she said in disbelief.

"Apologies, please ignore it," he said shortly. "It happens sometimes when I'm nervous."

Ignore it, he said. Fia wasn't sure how she was supposed to manage that. She could smell the cinnamon of his cologne much more strongly now she was this close to him, and she could see the awkwardness in the way he shifted his weight away from her. This was different from their previous encounters. This time, it was his turn to be awkward and uncomfortable, and she was the one with the chance to laugh at him - but suddenly, she found she didn't want to. Fia tried her best to control herself, in the end she just slipped one pinkie finger into a belt loop on his trousers and gave it a teasing tug.

"Unprofessional," she said.

"So sue me, I'm only human."

"But aren't you worried? You can't go on stage like that," she blinked up at him with wide concern in her eyes, but that just seemed to aggravate the man in front of her even more.

"What do you expect me to do about it?" he snapped out. The words hung for a moment in the silence of the elevator. "No," he added quickly. I don't mean-"

The atmosphere changed in that one instant. Later, Fia wouldn't know what had come over her. It wasn't the wine; she'd barely had a sip. Perhaps it was the frustrating way he spoke to her that pissed her off, or maybe she'd absorbed some of the tension he was vibrating with. It was as though someone else had taken over the movement of her body. She lifted her free hand, and drummed thoughtfully at the zip in front of her.

"Maybe we should take care of that," she said. She could feel the outline of him, and she gripped it gently. It was too big for her to cover with one hand. He hissed, and attempted to unpeel her fingers.

"No, I don't want-"

But she'd found a way to stop him talking, and she wanted to keep doing it now that she'd started; she wanted to break this annoying professional shell of his.

"Let me help, Sir," she said. "If you want it, just undo the button. Just undo it, and I can make this go away for you." She pressed her nose at the base of his outline and drew it upwards, kissing his tip through the expensive fabric. "I won't do anything unless you undo the button."

He moaned in the back of his throat. "I'm at work, we can't, there's a security camera- please, stop. I might not be able to calm myself, please. Everyone will be looking at me. They're all going to be looking at me."

Fia looked up into his darkening grey eyes. "It's only me looking at you now," she said, unfurling the umbrella at her feet and opening it. "Take it," she said softly and put it in his hands. "Don't let go."

CHAPTER NINE

It was above his head, enclosing them both in an even smaller space. It arched over the small ceiling of the elevator, blocking the cameras. He gripped the handle, his fingers blanching around it as she settled back on her heels.

"Undo the button," she said.

"What do you want?" The fingers on his other hand made flickering, aborted attempts towards his waistband. It wasn't enough. He hadn't given her permission yet. She wanted him to squirm.

"I want to taste you," she said with a smile. "I want to put you in my mouth." He choked a little, and she stroked him again as she continued, "I'll go slowly. Only the tip at first, I promise. Let me do that. I'll stop there if you want me to."

He said nothing for a moment, and his breath came shallowly as he made up his mind. Eventually he flipped the button undone in one quick movement. Fia drew the zipper down slowly, and watched the shape of him spill out above it. He sighed with the pressure gone. The head of his cock almost freed itself from the band of his briefs, and she kissed it again. It was warm. He almost whined.

She licked it. He held himself still, so very still. She circled her tongue around it, and felt his foreskin shift. Just as he started leaking, she covered the head of his cock with her mouth, and sucked. She almost felt him shudder, but it was barely there. She moved then, up and down; pinching his foreskin closed between her lips at his tip before she licked in between it with her tongue. He tasted like soap, and heat.

The umbrella shifted above her head, and Fia felt a hand cup the nape of her neck. She relaxed her mouth as he pushed her gently forwards, down and down until she felt blunt pressure at the back of her throat. He sighed.

"So good," he said. "It feels so good."

She hummed in agreement, and he twitched inside her.

Just then, the ringing in the background stopped as someone answered the call from the elevator emergency button. Fia tried to pull back, but a cradling hand at the back of her neck held her gently in place.

"Hello?" a voice came through the speakers above them. "Sorry for the delay. Are you okay in there?"

The heavy movement over Fia's tongue didn't stop, but it slowed for a moment and became more gentle. "We're stuck between floors eleven and twelve," he managed to answer. "Fix it, please. I've got somewhere to be."

"We're on it already – just resetting the system now – I'm sorry that you're uncomfortable. Give us ten minutes and we'll get you out."

But this obviously wasn't good enough for him. "Can't you work faster? I'm on a deadline," he said above her, frustration in every word. It wasn't necessary to be so rude. Fia bit down very slightly to teach him a lesson, and heard a slight sob in reply.

The sound was enough to concern the elevator operator, and he softened his voice, speaking soothingly. "It shouldn't be long now, stay calm," he said. "Everything will be fine if you can just find something else to think about. Just keep yourself occupied for a short while."

"Understood," he answered, and pressed the button again, closing the connection.

Fia pulled away from him then, twisting her hand around his length and using her saliva to ease the way. She looked up at him, at his face framed by the trembling umbrella.

"Ten minutes," she whispered, blowing on him gently. "Can you keep me busy for that long?"

He twitched from the cold. "Not a problem," he replied, thrusting forwards between her fingers. Fia laughed around him and cupped his balls, squeezing them in retaliation.

"Please," she said. "Please, Sir."

He couldn't speak after that; he couldn't reply to her whispered questions as she kissed his stomach and ran a thumb over his cock head; he could only stay silent as she sucked him, and concentrate on holding the umbrella still as he pushed forwards with his hips. He retreated to such a place of silent focus that Fia would have worried his mind had wandered if she hadn't looked up into his eyes; he couldn't take them away from her.

Soon he tried to withdraw, tapping her neck and running his thumb over her bottom lip. Fia refused to pay attention to him and gripped his hips tightly, unable to let him move away. She held him close as his cock seemed to swell for a moment, then his stomach hitched beneath his expensive shirt as he came, and her mouth filled with liquid and salt. She thought he might cry out, but he was still so silent. It was good to see every muscle in his body relax.

"Shit," he said. "Not on my trousers, please.

Help."

Fia smiled at him, and picked up her wineglass from the floor beside her. She looked up at him again, her blue eyes meeting his grey ones as she spat him out; one long line of white that fell into her remaining wine and dissolved. He reached out one trembling thumb and gently brushed it over the corner of her mouth before pushing it between her lips. She licked it clean as he noticed something on the doors. "Look," he said with subdued laughter, "A heart." He traced the outline of it.

Fia smiled, she'd forgotten about her heart. He refastened his trousers as the elevator began to move before re-furling the umbrella and returning it to her, trying not to look at her wine glass.

"I- we don't have any time-" he was struggling to come up with something to say, and this bothered her. Then she remembered drawing on the wall, she remembered her promise to appreciate herself more.

"You could say thank you, Sir," she said firmly. After all, she deserved it.

"Thank you," he shuddered slightly, re-adjusting his trousers as the elevator slowed and stopped at the ground floor. "I'm... much better now."

"I'm glad, Sir," Fia found herself saying. "Be good on the stage. I'll be watching you."

"I always am," he replied, the shield of his

sarcasm pulling back to him as the time to perform arrived.

He almost ran out of the elevator as soon as the door opened, brushing off the apologies of the workmen below it. He was soon lost in the crowd of the party.

"Where were you?" Louella took the umbrella from her, and gave it to Tony, who waved it above his head and grinned.

Fia struggled to adjust. Now she was out of the small space she could feel herself returning to take charge of her own body again, and she was beginning to realise the magnitude of what she'd just done. She tried to understand what had made her do it, but there were too many people around her, there was too much noise. She tried to focus on what Louella was saying.

"How long does it take to fetch an umbrella? Stop slacking off."

"It isn't even raining yet," she eventually managed to reply. "There's no rush."

"That's just as well," said Louella, "With your speed. Now, it's time for the boring speeches. We'd better go and watch them. The company insists we are there to boost the crowd numbers - heaven forbid the Partners don't look popular."

Fia nodded, and allowed herself to be pulled in the direction of the stage. It wasn't until they arrived at the front that she realised she still held the wine glass from the elevator, and it was too late to get rid of it now.

"You're too un-prepared," said Louella.

She jumped a little with guilt. "Am I?"

"You haven't brought any food with you to eat. We'll be here a while, and then you'll get tipsy on an empty stomach. Here," Louella held out a packet of biscuits, "Have some of these."

Fia took one and nibbled on it, trying to swallow around her bruised throat as the crowd built around them and their shoulders began to knock together. What would Louella think of her, if she knew what occurred ten minutes earlier? She must have been crazy. The waiting in silence didn't really help to keep her occupied, and she desperately tried to think about something else. Luckily, she was only just about to finish her biscuit when there was movement on the stage.

The MC walked on and began to crack jokes. Fia recognised him from some daytime television programme, but she couldn't remember which one. He congratulated them all on the award, Law firm of the year, and the crowd cheered as though it was the first time they'd won it, and not the fourth in a row. They were far too enthusiastic. Fia wondered what time they'd hit the free bar.

When the cheering died down he grew more

serious, and announced the arrival of the CEO of the company, who had come to speak to them. The audience responded with violent applause as a surprisingly familiar man walked onto the stage.

This was the moment Fia realised that she had made an error. It was entirely possible that the man she'd just had an encounter with in the elevator was slightly more important than she'd realised. She could remember the feel of his expensive suit, she could still taste him in her mouth, and now here he was, walking to the podium, carrying a large glass trophy that had been polished within an inch of its life. She glared at Louella.

"Who's he?" she hissed.

Her friend laughed disbelievingly. "You have got to be kidding me. That's Joel Bard, the CEO, you crazy woman. How could you not know who he is? I mean," she continued conversationally, eating another biscuit, "Technically he and Darby are equal partners, but Darby is too nice to make the hard decisions. No, it's that man in charge of all of us, for sure. Sometimes I think you live underneath a rock."

"But his office is only on the seventh floor! Don't the owners work from the penthouse?"

Louella shrugged. "He's not keen on heights," she said.

The man in charge was now raising a hand in the air, asking for quiet. The cheering died down. Fia didn't get a chance to reply, so she compromised by elbowing Louella hard in the ribs as he began his speech.

Joel Bard was a born performer. Fia couldn't see a hint of anxiety, or a trace of the tenseness that he'd carried with him only a moment earlier. Within two minutes, everyone in the audience was hanging on every word that dropped from his busy mouth. He walked the stage, using all of the available space and connecting with the audience on every side of the room - but his gaze always seemed to miss her. He thanked the individuals that had made the whole thing possible; he hoped that they would have a wonderful time at the party, because they deserved it. He carefully placed the trophy onto the podium and lifted a glass of champagne, inviting them all to join him in a toast.

Fia may as well be invisible. She felt her insides grow hot with the frustration of it: she'd compromised herself with her boss, and he didn't even seem to care. Had he even seen her in the audience? Was he ignoring her already? The audience raised their glasses too.

Fia took a step forwards, away from the mass of bodies beside her. She placed one finger into the remaining liquid in her wine glass and stirred, the cloudiness lifting from the bottom of it and incorporating with the wine. For a brief moment, the speech on the stage stuttered slightly, and the audience paused. Joel Bard's words began again, but weren't they almost hesitant?

He raised his champagne glass to his lips, the smile on his face forced. Fia raised her wine in response, and tipped it at him gently before drinking her own glass dry. Joel Bard choked instantly, and rapidly began a prolonged coughing fit as a waterfall of champagne darkened his collar.

He *was* looking at her, then. Good.

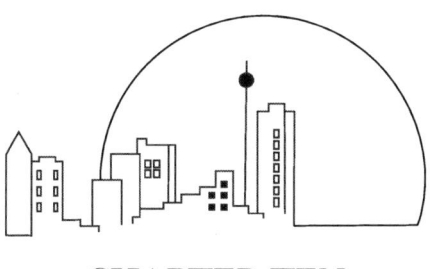

CHAPTER TEN

The hot spell finally broke, and the rainy season began. Tiny mists of raindrops coated the windows of the high rise, and the patters of rain at the windows gave small rounds of applause every time Fia learned a new skill. And she was learning quickly. Louella hadn't exaggerated when she spoke about the workload, and the paperwork.

Luckily, it was easy to find your way around the offices; the layout was identical on all of the floors except Darby's penthouse on the top floor, and the seventh floor. His cousin had taken half of it for his own office space, arranging it for the perfect view across the City. Fia found herself avoiding the seventh floor like the plague.

"What's got into you?" Louella had asked her

one day. "You'd think that floor had a bad smell, the way you wrinkle your nose when the elevator goes past it."

Fia shook her head, and replied that Lou was imagining things, but of course she wasn't. She *was* avoiding Joel Bard. Once the adrenaline of the moment had worn off, she couldn't look back at her behaviour without wincing - but she refused to curl up into a hot ball of embarrassment. He probably didn't want to talk to her either. She was doing them both a favour.

Their eyes only met again when he walked past reception a few days later. Luckily, they didn't need to talk; he was escorting company, and she had already learned that he never carried a key card with him. She just smiled a tight-lipped smile, and buzzed the gate. His guests talked amongst themselves as he stared at her.

She couldn't understand the look on his face; it fluctuated like the weather. One minute there was a spark in his eyes, and she felt heat wherever his gaze landed on her skin. The next, he was looking her over as if she was an opponent in court, his emotionless expression tearing her apart for any weaknesses. She suddenly felt unwelcome. Her finger was still on the buzzer, and the tinny hum came through the speaker next to her as the gate remained unlocked.

"Mr Bard?" the guests began to wonder about

the delay. He came to life at once.

"Forgive me. There's so much to do today, that I've already begun to think about it. This way." His face twitched up into his familiar professional smile, and he ushered them through the gate.

Fia removed her finger from the buzzer. There it was then, their first meeting since the incident in the elevator, and she had survived. It would get easier from now on, she was sure of it.

She managed to avoid him successfully after that. There were a few times when they passed each other in the corridor, and she left as wide a space as possible between them. He would flicker a smile at her that didn't quite reach his eyes, and she'd give him a small nod in return, but that was it.

It was always a pleasure to see Darby, though. She felt welcome in the building every time she saw him, knowing that he'd fought for her to have the job in the first place, and it diluted a lot of his cousin's strong feelings towards her.

"Fia!" he called to her one morning. "We need you. There are some clients in the meeting room that are proving... complicated. I'm worried we don't have enough back up in there. Could you come and take some notes for me? Louella says you have a faster writing speed than she does. We need to make sure we have every bit of information we can on this one."

"Sure," said Fia, her heart lifting. She collected a laptop and notepad, and followed him to the board room.

"Come in quietly," he warned her. "The meeting has already started." He pushed open the door with a quiet hush, and they went inside.

Her eyes widened as she recognised the clients inside it: she saw the mother of the little boy abandoned in reception, and the man sitting opposite her was obviously her husband. Fia didn't know whether the Bard cousins had persuaded her to come back to the company with bribery or with blackmail, but at least she was here.

Joel Bard sat at the head of the table, his dark black suit making the room even more sombre. Darby joined him, for once looking as grim as his cousin did. The atmosphere was thick, like tar. You wouldn't even be able to cut it with a knife; it was dense, and clingy.

Fia sat at the far end of the long table and flipped open her laptop, burying her head behind the screen. She really hoped that they'd all soon forget that she was there, and so she said nothing and began to type as soon as they started talking again. She'd obviously come in mid-conversation.

"I don't understand why you keep talking about it," said the mother. "I'm a woman, not just a parent. *I'm* applying to be your client, and I'm the one with needs – why do you keep talking about the boy? What about *my* priorities?"

"Let's just figure out a safe place for the boy first, and then we can get to all your needs," said Darby with a smile.

"I want to separate the assets quickly; I want to travel abroad by the end of the year. I've brought a list -" The woman held out a paper, and her hand trembled slightly as it vibrated above the table. No one made a move to take it, and so she just let go. It floated gently down onto the table like an abandoned autumn leaf.

"We can't represent you; you know that. We're not here to help you divorce, just to reunite you with your son," said Joel Bard, in a more reasonable voice than Fia had ever heard him use. His expression didn't match his tone, though, and she wondered how long he would be able to hold it together.

"I don't want him."

"Do you even care where your son is? What home he's in, what he had for breakfast?"

"You both have a reputation for kind heartedness, so I know the boy is safe. I've got no reason to worry." The woman sat back in her chair and attacked her manicure with a well-used nail file. "Darby Bard is a kind family man, isn't he? I knew you'd look after him - I'm not that terrible."

"But unfortunately, it's not really in our job description," said Darby, ruefully. "You can't hire us for childcare – and you chose to have the little fellow, after all. He's a lovely child. We both think you're lucky to have him."

"I won't do it – and why do you keep looking at me, anyway? His father is an equal parent, so why am I considered the bad one in this situation, answer me that? It's time he looked after him for a change."

"You want the boy's father to take over?" asked Darby, a beat later.

"I demand it."

Fia finished typing the mother's bald reply, and looked at the husband, who had remained silent up until now. She wasn't the only one to do so, and when he had the attention of everyone in the room, he finally spoke.

"This has nothing to do with me. I'll talk about the divorce, but don't mention the brat."

"So," Joel Bard tapped a finger against the leg of his chair. "Let's understand this. You're both denying all responsibility for your child – but while I might sympathise with your feelings, I don't feel we are getting anywhere today. After all, the boy has to live with *someone*."

But it would be better if he was wanted, thought Fia, her fingers skimming over the keyboard as she wrote all of this down. He needs to be safe, and loved. She looked at the hard eyes of the mother as she refused to respond, and winced.

Darby sighed. "If you don't want to discuss this with each other in the room, we can set up different meetings-"

"No," said the woman. "I won't come back here again; I don't need to. Surely any idiot could understand what my wishes are by now. His father is in the room; it's time he stepped up. If he cares for his son for the next five years we'll only be equal, after all. Children are fucking expensive."

The husband reached his breaking point at this, and shoved at the table, which rocketed forwards and caught his wife across her midriff. She curled in on herself with a cry, and began to retch. Darby shot out an arm and took her by the elbow to steady her; he was bending over her and checking she was all right. His cousin grabbed the back of the husband's chair and dragged it backwards by a metre, standing in front of it and caging him in.

"None of that," he said. "We're not starting anything physical. I can understand that you're angry, but she has a point. He's your child too."

The husband's face screwed up in anger as he tried to break free of the chair. "No, he damn well isn't," he shouted, one shaky finger pointed at the woman opposite. "I had a DNA test done – all those work trips, and the boy looks nothing like me. She's a liar. He's not my son."

Darby let go of the mother, who slumped back in her chair and finally fell silent. The husband finally managed to get back to the table, picking up a paper and throwing it at Joel Bard. He caught it, and scanned the document, reading the DNA results, his mouth now set in one thin line of tense anger.

"Why would you test that?" screamed the mother, completely beside herself.

"Because you're a liar! You sit here, in this room, demanding I take care of your son when you know he isn't mine!"

Fia's fingers flew over the keys on her laptop as she struggled to keep up with everything that was being mentioned, but all she really wanted to do was pause and figure out what was going on. Things were beginning to get a little confusing, even for her. And then –

"I didn't say *my husband*," said the woman. "I said, his *father*."

Fia stopped typing mid-sentence, and tried to make sense of that. She didn't think the husband had understood it either, because he was becoming more and more irate.

"If I hadn't found out myself, would you ever have told me?" he demanded. "Would you have expected me to raise the brat?"

"You wouldn't raise him anyway; do you think

I don't know that? You never wanted children - that's why I'm doing this!"

"And so, you just thought you'd give away the proof of your infidelity, and I wouldn't leave you? That I'd just thank you for it and what, buy you a drink? Good luck with that plan, darling."

"I've been nothing but good to you!"

"Good? You couldn't even manage to be faithful - any woman in the world would be better than you," her husband snorted. "I have no idea why you think yourself difficult to replace. This one here would do. Are you single, sweetheart? Do you lie to people?"

He was behind Fia's chair now. She hoped he couldn't read the notes she'd taken. As she covered the screen of her laptop, he rested his hot hands on her shoulders and squeezed, before running them down her arms and hugging her tight, rubbing her against his chest.

"I've got a lot of money," he crooned into her hair. "Women like that, don't they?"

"Let go of me," Fia whispered, her skin crawling, knowing that her self-defence classes were going to be useless here. She'd probably get sacked immediately if she hit a client.

Joel Bard slammed the DNA report back onto the table, and shot him a murderous look. The pressure on Fia's shoulders was suddenly gone, and the husband was pressed against the wall on the opposite side of the room.

"Oh," said Fia in surprise. Maybe she would have got away with it after all.

No one moved for a moment, the mother in pain at the table, the husband flat against the wall, and Joel Bard next to him with one muscled arm across his throat. For a moment Fia hovered there, unsure of what to do, until the tension was broken by the expert skills of Darby Bard.

He looked ruefully at Fia. "Can you fetch us some coffee?" he asked. "Black, two sugars. I think we all need an energy boost to get through all of this."

Fia nodded, grateful for the dismissal. She ran out of the room.

There was a tiny kitchen at the end of the corridor, tucked into one corner of the floor. It had two cupboards in it, one full of identical cream cups that were used when company came, and one with miss-matched mugs that sported football team logos and cartoon characters that everyone used the rest of the time. Fia chose one with a violently red Christmas robin on it; she was thirsty too after all that drama. She ran it under the cold tap as the kettle boiled to remove the dust, and it joined the line of polite white crockery that she set out for the meeting.

Paul would have loved this robin, it looked as

though it hated the holiday season – he used to say that colour was everything, and this colour red was angry with the world.

As she set the mug down, she heard the snick of the door opening and closing.

"Are you alright?"

It was Joel Bard. He'd followed her from the meeting room. This was the first time he'd spoken to her since that night at the party, since she'd found out who he was. It looked like she was the only one taking the time to feel awkward about it, because he wandered around the kitchen with the same loose-muscled walk as ever.

"Is the client meeting over?" she asked.

"No. It's not going well, to be honest, but Darby is better at crowd control than I am. He'll sort it. I'll go back in a moment. I came to see if you were okay."

Fia's shoulders were still in one tense line since that man had touched them. "I'm fine," she said.

"You look stressed. I understand that. I feel the same; this job can really get to you on some days. I'm sorry."

Short, clipped sentences. A robotic voice. It was hard to believe this was the same man who spoke so eloquently on stage not so long ago; he seemed incapable of making a sentence last more than three seconds when he was around her.

"I don't want that little boy going home with either of those awful people. He needs to be with a family that loves him."

Footsteps stopping behind her and a tense sigh. She could smell Joel Darby's cologne. His hands were at her waist, pinching her hips. His breath warmed the back of her neck.

"I agree with you, now that I've seen them. Godawful people, the both of them. I hope Darby gets some kind of answer today."

"Hmm," she said

"I'll help with the coffee. Don't go back in there," he said. Fia didn't reply, and he laughed a little. "You're a quiet one," he commented. "Quiet, but difficult to ignore. How do you manage that?"

He pushed his torso into hers, brushing the hardness of his erection against her as she turned around to look at him, using the friction of her movement for a whisper of pleasure and humming in approval. Fia glanced over at the door. It didn't have a lock - this was hardly private. She tried to step back from his contact but the counter-top began to dig into the dip of her lower back. His warm body held her firmly against the granite of it.

"Why are you like this now?" she asked, tipping her pelvis away from him.

"Because I'm fucking *angry*. They're being

106

bastards in there, and I just can't concentrate any more. I need to calm down. Please."

Fia placed one hand on his chest and managed to push him back a few centimetres, buying herself a bit of distance. He was as rude as she remembered, and she suddenly wanted to teach him a lesson; she wanted him to realise that he wasn't always the most important person in the room. He clasped her hand and moved it down his chest, down below his belt buckle and pressed it into him.

"Please," he said again.

"What do you want?" Fia watched him swallow, his neck muscles tightening briefly as he considered her question.

"I need you," he replied shortly.

"To do what?"

"Please," he said again, drawing out the word, making it sound sarcastic. "Quickly. Calm me down. It has to be now. I have to get back – I can't go in like this."

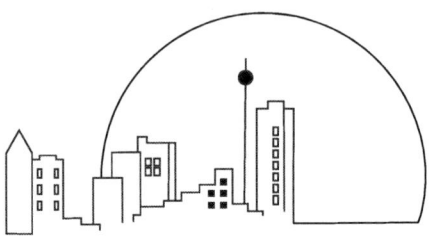

CHAPTER ELEVEN

He smelled too good. Fia didn't want to argue with him. She spat into one hand and slid her fingers flat, down across his stomach and into his trousers. Her hands were still freezing cold from the tap but he didn't care; he barely winced as she gripped him. She rolled the weight of him around her fingers experimentally, and then twisted her wrist and pulled.

"Yes. Harder." His head fell to rest on her shoulder, his nose at her collar-bone. He keened as she sped up her movements, and she shushed him.

"Quiet," she whispered into his ear. "You're doing so well. I need you to come for me."

"Yes," he whispered back, cupping her breasts so hard that they blanched. Her neckline rode down, and one nipple peeped over it. He bit down on it, and

Fia hissed in a breath at the slight pain that bloomed across her chest. He was chasing her movements now, his hips pushing forward when she moved her hand towards him. It was a tight space. Her wrist barely fit inside his still-buttoned trousers and her movements were rough and small. She wondered if she was hurting him.

He came just as the kettle clicked off the boil. Fia's hand was hot and sticky, trapped inside the cotton of his boxers. She removed it once his shudders had stopped and licked one finger gently. He still tasted the same.

"Stop that, woman," he whispered. Gentle fingers smoothed her blouse, returning her neckline to its original position. "Wash your hands, there's a sink right there."

The sound of tinkling crockery as she did just that, a spoon stirring against porcelain. Fia stood by the sink and watched her boss make the coffee with the same high level of concentration that he did everything else with. He placed all the white cups onto a tray as she stared at him. He misunderstood her confusion, and thought she was asking for something.

"Thank you,' he said.

Fia didn't reply. He tipped a small smile at her then, and Fia realised that whatever storm of emotions he had come in with had gone.

"Are we going to be friends?" she asked, truly curious about the answer.

"I don't tend to make friends."

So, it would be like that then. "I'm very hard to please, anyway," she said. "You'd never qualify."

"You must have so many," he huffed, pushing the robin mug across the kitchen work surface. She ignored it.

He left as quietly as he had arrived, closing the door behind him. She was alone in the kitchen again.

Why on earth had she broken the promise that she'd made to herself - she wasn't going to touch him again, was she? Well, that had lasted less than a week. No self-control, she thought, and such a selfish man. He'd left her wet with no relief.

She reached beneath her skirt and removed her soaked panties, balling them up in frustration and burying them at the bottom of her handbag, before picking up the robin mug and taking a sip. At least he'd made her coffee.

A dash of almond milk and one sweetener, she thought in surprise. He knew the way she took her coffee. That was... unexpected. She took another sip. It was good. He rose very slightly in her estimation.

Fia didn't need him to be a friend, after all. She had others, and she decided to go and visit one at the weekend, to remind herself of that fact. It took her an hour in the car with all the traffic, and she knew she was getting close when the scenery began to change.

There were no high rises on the outskirts of the city. Instead, small single-level houses were packed in together, and their small gardens behind the low fences were brown and dead. The rainy season hadn't had a chance to bring them back to life yet, and no one around here could afford sprinklers.

Fia hadn't been back to the suburbs since her brother had died, and it looked as though life had completely paused here while she was away. She drove her dented Micra through the quiet streets, curving it gently around the potholes until she stopped the engine outside a warehouse with giant blue doors and put the handbrake on. She was just getting out of the car when a woman in dungarees came over to the passenger window, kicking up dirt with her worn-out boots.

"I'm sorry, we're closed at the moment, can I help you?" she called through the glass.

Fia rolled the window down. "Hello, Susie."

The woman stared at her for a full minute until recognition set in, and tears filled her eyes. "Fia? Fia! is it really you? Come out, come out, come in!" she said, as she herded her out of the car and through the blue doors. Fia ran a hand over them as she passed; they were as badly painted as she remembered. "I haven't seen you since-"

The funeral, thought Fia. This is the first time I've ever seen you without Paul being in the room. She should have come back earlier. Her brother's girlfriend was obviously pleased to see her.

Susie chattered non-stop. How was Fia doing? Was she still writing? Did she melt completely in the hot season this year, it was terrible wasn't it? Fia smiled, and let her come to a stop before she spoke.

"You still run the art classes, then," she said.

The room was filled with low tables covered in paper and pots of paint. Heaped brushes lay piled up in the sinks, splats of colour covered the floor of the warehouse. The space was surprisingly silent; the children had just gone home.

"I do." Susie put her hands in her pockets and surveyed the mess. "Paul would have wanted it all to carry on. But look at the state of the place; I'll be here until midnight."

"I'll help you clean," Fia said.

Susie smiled. "I'll fetch you some dungarees. You look untouchable in those clothes. And there's a pair of your glasses that you left here somewhere. I'll recognise you again then."

It took several hours to return some state of organisation to the room. Fia had plenty of time to think while she flicked congealed paint from the brush bristles and watched it collect in the basin. She collected the damp papers from the tables and hung the children's pictures on pegs to dry.

The tables gradually cleared, and a swag of colourful painted bunting zigzagged across the ceiling. Fia felt more like herself than she had for a long time, now she was back in her battered trainers with her hair scraped back, and she attacked the stains on the table tops, the smell reminding her of her brother.

It was good to be in a place like home. JD Bard and Associates had managed to crawl too far underneath her skin, both the company and the CEO himself. She didn't quite know why she was so angry with Joel Bard, or why she couldn't walk away from him when he looked at her in that particular way; why she couldn't damp down the heat that rose up inside, when he wanted her. They weren't compatible at all - all they did was argue.

But that's it, she thought suddenly, rinsing out the final pot and placing it on the side to drain. He lets me argue back. Paul can't answer me anymore, and I'm not listened to when I try to publish my book, but when I get stern with Joel Bard, he just takes it.

And she couldn't entirely blame him for his opinion of her, not when she thought about her behaviour over the last month. The situation seemed unfixable. Fia viciously chipped away at the dry paint stuck to the tap, and decided that it didn't even matter. Who wanted to get closer to such a cold man?

It was just a bit of fun. She was only going to be there for a year, and then she just knew she'd be writing again. Maybe she'd make him a character in one of her books, and then kill him off spectacularly in the final scene. She'd enjoy that.

The sun had long set when the women both swirled mops around the floor, talking to each other through the rising scent of disinfectant. Susie brought her a glass of lemonade when they were finally done, and they sat down on the floor together. She was holding a square packet, which she placed gently down onto the floor and pushed towards Fia with an apologetic look on her face.

"I was hoping you'd come back," she said. "I didn't know how to get in touch with you. This is yours – Paul left it with me. He was very proud of it. I know it's unfinished, but I wanted to return it to its rightful home."

Fia un-wrapped the stained brown paper, and took a small book from it. She flipped through the pages. Leaf after leaf of colourful drawings, her own words scattered through them. The last few pages were blank. She saw an ink splash on the front cover, and wiped it gently with one thumb. It was a useless gesture. The ink had dried over eighteen months ago; she remembered Paul's wry face and the language he'd used when he'd dropped the brush on it.

This was the prototype of their last book. The original that they'd once worked on together. Hours of memories washed over her in one quick minute, and for a while she couldn't speak. She nodded her head once, and Susie recognised a 'thank you'.

She smiled. "Will you come back another day? You could read to the children. They used to love your stories."

"I don't do that at the moment," said Fia shortly.

"Why not?"

"I get sick. I don't know why. I try and look at the words, but they just move." Her lip began to tremble.

Susie rubbed her shoulder and hummed in sympathy. "Listen, I'm sorry, about the book, I heard about the lawsuit. I wondered if this was the right time to return it to you, but I wasn't sure when you'd find a moment to visit me again."

"No, that's all right. I'm glad to have it." Fia tucked it into her bag with a watery smile.

"Be kinder to yourself. You did your best to finish it well. It must have been hard to try and replace your brother - I know that more than anyone, right?"

Fia just nodded, and hugged her. For a moment Susie looked as fragile as she was, but she hid it quickly.

"Maybe you should follow all the advice I keep getting. The past is the past - if it seems unfixable, start again on a new day. Keep the memories, but write another book."

Fia took a drink of lemonade and concentrated on the bubbles popping on her tongue. "But half of the illustrations were Paul's. He worked so hard on it; I can't let it go."

"Something is always left unfinished when an artist goes. He wouldn't want you to fret over it," said Susie firmly. "Paul would say to move on."

"Have you?"

"I've started to try, at least. And I keep busy. My family keep talking about blind dates – I expect I won't be able to say no in a year or so."

"We should go on a night out," said Fia suddenly. "Soon. I'll invite Louella. You might have to listen to a little bit of legal talk, but I'll try to keep her to a minimum."

Susie smiled again, but this time it was pure amusement. "That sounds great. But now it's time to go home. It's getting late, and you have work tomorrow, right?"

Fia stood up, her legs a little numb from sitting cross-legged on the floor. "I'll help you carry your supplies home," she said.

"You don't need-"

"Paul would tell me to," she interrupted. "Come on."

The short walk to Susie's apartment only took five minutes. The rain began to spot as they said goodbye, and Fia began the return walk to her car. She recognised every other front door and wondered whether the same families lived behind them, confirming it when she saw the same old cars in the driveways. When she was half way back she realised that the memories didn't hurt in quite the same way that they used to.

The rain began to consider falling in earnest as she searched for her car keys, and just as the heavens opened she realised that they were locked inside the art building along with her mobile phone. She'd forgotten them when she'd left with Susie.

A few seconds later she was completely drenched from head to toe in cold water, and her hands slipped on the padlock and chain as she checked them for any give. It was locked up tight.

Her hair was plastered to her head, and her clothes were soaked. Fia had no choice but to brave the weather, but she decided not to go back to Susie's apartment, reluctant to worry her still-grieving friend. Instead, she would walk to the nearest bus stop on a route that headed into the City, and find her own way home. Her car would be perfectly safe here until tomorrow; she knew that if the weather didn't put off the car thieves, then the large dents in it would.

The borrowed dungarees flapped against her legs as she walked, and her glasses were smeared with rain water. She rubbed at her arms to lower the goose bumps that had risen all over her body and tried not to shiver; the water was running into her mouth now, and she swallowed it. Every now and then a car would pass her and its headlights would illuminate the wall of water that was falling from the sky.

Fia just concentrated on putting one sodden foot in front of the other. Soon she was surrounded by small shops and businesses as she entered a busier part of the city, a place she had visited with Paul and Susie during better times. She knew there used to be a bus stop here, right outside a burger joint and a small delicatessen. Things didn't change quickly in this part of town, so her hopes were high. The deli was closed of course, but she could see the neon hamburger sign at the end of the street.

The bus stop had no shelter, and so Fia had no chance to get out of the rain. She examined the little paper stuck onto the signpost, and saw that the last bus had departed twenty minutes earlier. She had no way home. She felt a hot sob rising and choked it back; she pretended that the warm tears in her eyes were from the boiling storm clouds above her.

The lock turned in the burger joint doorway, and the sign on it flipped to 'closed'. The neon sign

politely blinked out. The only illumination in the
street now came from a car parked illegally outside it
with the engine running. It was too dark, too late at
night and too dangerous. You were too on edge after
seeing all those memories, she scolded herself. You
wanted to walk, to burn energy, and look where it's
got you. A shiver contracted through her entire body,
not all of it from the cold.

She examined the car, trying to place it as
friend or foe. Water rolled from its waxed and shiny
roof, and she could hear opera music leaking through
the metal. It couldn't be more out of place. It was a
shiny Mercedes, parked where it shouldn't be. Oh,
and then she recognised it.

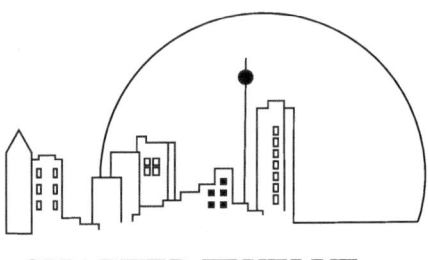

CHAPTER TWELVE

Despite every fibre of her hating the idea of Joel Bard seeing her like this, Fia was out of options; her body temperature must be dangerously low by now, and he was a safer bet than a stranger. Too freezing cold to care what he thought of her drowned appearance, she walked up to it and knocked on the driver's door. The window cracked by an inch.

"Sir?" she asked.

The window unrolled quickly with just this one word. It's a password, she thought. A secret code. She blinked at him through her wet glasses.

"Get in," he said, and he unlocked the passenger door.

Once inside, Fia could get a better sense of the storm. The rain drummed on the roof so loudly that it was no wonder the music was turned up so high. He turned it down now until it was just a quiet background of soprano. Her seat was already damp.

"Thank you," she said.

"A pleasure. Although I am intrigued – how the hell did you know this was my car?"

"I'm stalking you," she said, completely deadpan. If he didn't recognise her, this was not the moment to remind him of it. She didn't know what he would do if he remembered their first encounter, and she needed to get home.

"You know I organise restraining orders for a living, right?"

Fia just dried her glasses and put them back on, which allowed Joel Darby to come into sharp focus – he was sitting in the driver's seat and eating a dirty burger meal.

"My, how fancy," she said, leaning over and stealing a chip.

He shrugged, unconcerned. "Life can't all be lobster and caviar. If you promise not to tell on me you can have another chip."

She took one; it had been a long time since lunch and she was starving. When she checked the clock on the dashboard she saw that it was gone midnight.

"You look different." He leaned forward and stared at her face. She flinched slightly as he reached forward and rubbed gently at her chin. "What have you been painting today? I don't mind the water, but I draw the line at paint. Don't get any on the upholstery."

Fia pulled away from him and reached for the seatbelt, buckling it tight. "Can you give me a ride? I'm stranded."

"Where do you live?"

She told him. He watched her shiver, and listened to her stomach rumble. His eyes narrowed. "My place is closer. Let's get you dry first, and then I'll take you home. Here," he tipped the remaining half of the burger meal onto her lap and put the car into gear. "Eat that, my hands are busy. We need to get you out of those clothes."

He fell silent as he pulled away from the curb, and Fia was too grateful to be rescued to lecture him on his terrible parking. She simply listened to the woman's voice coming sad and strong through the speakers, and ate his food.

Joel Bard lived in a ground floor apartment. Fia was amused, despite her shivers. This was a gorgeous old building with wrought iron balconies. The view from any one of them would be stunning.

"Does it have gargoyles?" she asked.

"No." He opened the door and waited for her, but she was too busy looking at the architecture.

He put one hand on the small of her back and steered her through it. "And I know the rain's died down but I'd like to get inside. You may already be soaked, but I'm not."

"Wouldn't you rather have a balcony?"

"No."

Fia dripped dirty rainwater onto the thick pile of the cream rug in his entranceway. She left a trail of it behind her as he showed her into the living space. Everything was white; white walls, cream sofas and steel beams. White orchids peeped at her from the windowsills. It was beautiful, but stark. She felt like a cartoon character in her baggy dungarees splattered in bright paint.

"Don't sit on anything."

Fia nodded. She'd already decided that on her own, thank you very much. "You have a lovely home," she said awkwardly, wondering for the hundredth time whether there was something wrong with her. Her words were as vanilla as her environment. "I still think you'll regret not having a view out over the City though," she added pettishly.

He shrugged. "I can move apartments if I do. I own the building." He pointed at a door. "You want that one, it's the bathroom. Take a robe, dry yourself and get warm. I'm not taking you to the hospital if you collapse."

Fia pointed to the door next to it. "What's that

one?" she said.

"My bedroom," he said, tilting his head to one side and looking at her.

Fia stopped asking questions at once, and headed firmly in the direction of the bathroom. Once the door was safely closed she stripped out of her wet clothes, and left them in the sink - she couldn't think of anywhere else to put them. After trying to wipe the mascara circles away from beneath her eyes she gave up, and stepped beneath the hot shower.

The bottles in the bathroom all smelled like Joel Bard. She spent some time breathing in their dark cinnamon scent but decided she wouldn't use them -she didn't want to smell like him. It was bad enough that she was here in the first place. She simply waited for the heat to chase away her chill and her shivers to stop, and then she shut the water off; she'd been wet for long enough already. As her feet sank into the fluffy bath mat she saw that there was a dryer in the bathroom, and so she posted her wet clothes inside it and started a cycle, pulling on a bathrobe that she found hanging on the back of the door. It was warm, fluffy heaven.

Fia knew she shouldn't let her boss see her like this, but she was too exhausted to care. She needed to sit down before she fell down, and so she hugged the robe firmly around her and fastened it tight before padding back out to the living space in bare feet. The thick layer of cotton didn't feel like enough protection. Stay away from him, she thought. Don't let him within arm's length of you.

Fia's awkwardness fell by the wayside when she saw Joel Bard flickering through paperwork on the coffee table, placing it into one neat pile. He was already working.

"I shan't apologise for the mess; you weren't invited. You'll have to take me as you find me. I have paperwork coming out of my ears as usual," he said.

Fia sat on the sofa to dry her hair. "I can help?

The laugh he gave offended her. "No, thank you. It's very sensitive information. Do you think you're the perfect person to trust with it?"

"I think I'm the best person for you to trust with it." Fia peeped at him through her towel.

"Do tell me why."

"Because you're already worried about the amount that I know about you, and the people I could talk to about your behaviour at work. How bad could it get now?"

"You should have been a lawyer," he said grimly, shutting it away into a cabinet.

Fia picked up one forgotten page from the sofa, and balanced her glasses on her nose to read it. Before she could get a proper glance, Joel Bard snatched it from her fingers. He smiled before she could get angry, and flicked her on the nose.

"I said no, learn to listen. This isn't something you can help with."

"I've got more skills than you realise," she grumbled.

And now he was too close. She shifted away from him to the far end of the sofa, and he looked at the tip of his finger as though he had burned it.

"I'm beginning to think you're more complicated that I first imagined, actually," he said, pouring a measure of whiskey into a heavy crystal glass. "You look very different today."

He offered the glass to her, but Fia shook her head. Alcohol at this point would just send her to sleep, and she knew she had to keep her wits about her.

"You seem different too," she replied with thought, as he joined her on the sofa. He sat respectfully at the other end of it and sipped his whiskey, but it still seemed too close. She tucked the dressing gown more firmly around her and wondered how long the dryer would take. "I didn't see you as a knight in shining armour. Although I am grateful," she added quickly when she saw the expression on his face. "You just have a different reputation at work, that's all."

"Really? Do tell." He took another sip and

looked at her with a challenge.

Fia suddenly didn't want to answer him. She certainly couldn't tell him the real answer to his question; he wouldn't like that at all. "That you're a workaholic," she said after a while.

"I am. What else?"

Fia gave up the pretence. "That you're rude to people. And selfish," she said.

"How ungrateful." He tutted. "I think I'm more polite than you are."

He was needling her, and it was working.

"You are selfish, though," she muttered under her breath. He stiffened, and she knew he'd heard her.

"Evidence?"

"Evidence based on personal interactions." Fia shifted uncomfortably on the sofa cushions.

A look of understanding shot through Joel Bard's features, and his eyebrows rose. "With you?" He shifted closer to her, tipping her chin towards him with gentle knuckles that smelled faintly of alcohol.

Fia hummed a yes at him, and pulled her chin away. She pulled the glass in his other hand towards her and took a fiery sip while she tried to process the expression on his face. He grinned wickedly at her.

"I understand. I'm a bad person, then. I've come twice, and you haven't. What should we do about that?"

CHAPTER THIRTEEN

He took another drink and leaned forwards, brushing her nose with his before pressing his mouth down on her lips. It wasn't really a kiss, she realised. He parted her mouth with his tongue and pressed inwards, releasing another wave of neat whiskey. She swallowed around his tongue and felt the hot burn of it in the back of her throat, warming up the last bit of her that was still frozen from the storm.

A strong grip around her waist, and another at the nape of her neck. He pulled her onto his lap, her robe riding up as she straddled his knee. Fia felt him lean her head to one side, and a cold stream of whiskey ran down her neck and pooled above her breasts.

"I should pay my dues," he whispered,

drinking his own mouthful, suckling downwards from behind her ear to her shoulder. She whimpered and he shushed her, kneading her behind as he rutted her up and down on his thigh, the expensive weave of his suit pulling roughly at her.

"Good woman," he said. "Get my trousers wet. Ruin them for me, beautiful."

And she was wet. The shot of whiskey added to her exhaustion, giving her a buzz that she felt everywhere, but that soon centred between her thighs. She had experienced just too many emotions today, and she was wrecked. He increased the friction, rubbing circles above her hips as he moved her up and down in a perfect rhythm. She was soon lost in it.

And he seemed to be lost as he looked at her. His hold on her loosened, but Fia continued to ride him, caught up in the rhythm of the sensation. He stroked her damp pubic hair lightly before pressing down firmly.

"Come for me, then," he said, and Fia shuddered as she followed his order. He cradled her lightly as she rode it out, and then laid her down onto the sofa.

She blinked up at him, all arousal in her eyes.

"When you look at me like that, you make this so easy," he said, biting gently at her ear. "That was one," he whispered into it.

He parted the robe beneath the belt that she'd

tied so firmly against him earlier, and licked her. Fia cried out then, pressing her hands to her mouth to drown out the sound.

"Maybe I should evict the neighbours," he whispered. "Then you can make as much noise as you like, troublesome woman."

She had no breath to reply to him. She was sobbing before he nuzzled upwards, sucking her clit firmly as she came once more, her head thrown back into the sofa cushions. It was almost clinical brutality; a challenge completed. Fia had come twice, and the debt was paid.

When her senses returned to her, Joel Bard was sitting beside her, sipping his whiskey, his breathing uneven. She ran an exploring ankle over his lap. He was very, very hard.

"You haven't-"

"That wasn't the plan."

Fia sat up slowly, her muscles still shaking slightly. She felt at her rapidly-drying hair that was knotting up beautifully. Great. He huffed in amusement, and pulled a comb from his jacket pocket, beginning to drift it through the tangles. All of Fia's muscles felt as though they were made of warm butter.

"Thank you," she said, but whether that was for the hair care or the orgasms she wasn't quite sure.

She felt him half-laugh behind her again. "A

gentleman pays his debts," he said.

"Ah, transactional to a fault," Fia replied.

She knew what this was. Attraction, yes – but just useful in the moment. They only seemed to argue, after all. The atmosphere was always tense between them. Until now, she realised. She was comfortable, relaxed. She counted the twists as he braided her hair. When had he learned to do that? An ex-girlfriend maybe, or a sister. She knew nothing about him. Suddenly she felt she should ask him to tell her something about himself, now he was relaxed, and she had the chance of an answer.

"Why the ground floor?" she asked. "Do you really have a problem with heights?"

There was a pause, but after a moment he actually began to answer her.

"I was stuck on the side of a mountain for several hours, as a child. It was... cold. I held onto the rock for as long as I could, but I remember that as my fingers began to freeze, my grip loosened. I nearly fell - I'm very lucky that my family found me when they did."

"That's awful."

"Well, my family have always been keen on ambitious holidays. We had to be seen as progressive, someone to aspire to. I never believed in all of that, to be honest. Darby found me, in the end. We've always looked out for each other."

"Oh." Fia didn't know what else to say; she was surprised he'd told her, and the expression on his face seemed to show how surprised he was, that he had.

Joel Bard gently tugged the hair tie from her wrist, and fastened it into the back of her braid, as though he'd done it for someone a hundred times before. He tucked the loose strands behind her ears, and circled his fingers at the base of her neck.

Shifting backwards she felt his erection pressing into her back. He didn't seem to want to do anything about it. It was the environment that drove him to sex then, not her. This beautiful man didn't want to be personal, and she tried not to let it offend her. She was here now, and she would only think of now.

And he *was* beautiful like this, balanced on an edge and pretending he was fine. Fia felt a twitch of interest in her abdomen, and she ran a hand up his leg, still soaking wet. She'd done that. She felt the outline of him through his trousers.

"Sir-" she cupped his face, her eyes just inches from his own now, her breath mixing with his as she watched his pupils dilate.

"Yes?"

"I want..." What did she want? Fia wasn't sure.

"I-" He hesitated. He reached for the bow at

her waist, finally loosening her robe and pushing it away from her shoulders. His lips were barely brushing hers when his phone rang. He pulled back instantly to answer it, and Fia felt strangely cold.

"Hello?" his voice was clipped, professional. There was no hint of friendship in it. "Yes, of course. I'll be there as soon as I can. The judge won't arrive until ten; we have plenty of time." He stood as he terminated the call. "I have to go," he said to Fia, tucking one final strand of hair behind her ear. He didn't seem to register doing it at all, and he barely noticed when she wrapped the bathrobe back around herself. "I have to get back to the office. I have to change - I'll get your clothes."

Fia remembered the state of his trousers, and blushed. Her clothes were warm from the dryer when he handed them to her, and then he disappeared back into the bathroom. She was fully dressed before he came back out, and she couldn't understand what was taking him so long, but then she suddenly remembered how hard he was before the phone call. He must be taking care of himself - he couldn't go out like that. Suddenly she wanted to see him; to see his face when he finally came.

That wouldn't be possible behind a locked door, but maybe she could hear him. The oak of the bathroom door was too thick for her to make out much as she held an ear to it - she thought she could make out one loud intake of breath, but she wasn't sure. By the time he came out in an entirely new suit, buttoning the cuffs of his shirt, she was back sitting innocently on the sofa.

"Are you ready to go?"

"I don't want to cause you further trouble; you'll be late to the office. I'll just order a taxi," Fia offered awkwardly. "I live in the opposite direction."

"I don't have time to wait for a taxi."

"Go first, then. I'll be safe here. It will only take fifteen minutes or so to get here."

"I'll drive you," he said firmly.

"Why?" Fia asked with a laugh. "Are you worried I'll go through all your notes while you're gone?" Once the silence had gone on for too long, her face fell. "Oh God, you are. You really don't trust me at all."

"Please don't get upset."

"Is it something that terrible? Will you be in a lot of trouble if the information in that folder gets out?"

"No. You know I have a duty to keep this private, you've worked at the company for long enough now. You're getting upset for no reason - it's not personal."

"I know that nothing that's happened this evening is personal, thank you," she replied quietly.

He didn't answer. He just stood there quietly,

holding his car keys. The mood in the room had hung on an edge from the moment the phone rang, and now it completely soured. Fia stood up immediately and opened the front door.

"Let's go," she said.

The ride back to her tiny apartment took place in complete silence. Fia tried to remain sitting up ramrod straight and offended, but the memories she'd re-lived, the cold and the orgasms had exhausted her, and she drifted off to sleep before they were half way there. Joel Bard gave her shoulder a tiny shake when they were outside her front door.

"You're home," he said quietly. Fia opened her eyes with a moment's confusion. "Don't come in early tomorrow, get some rest. I'll send someone to collect your car and keys in the afternoon." She tried to protest, but he spoke over her. "Don't argue. I need my employees to be reliable, and you need to be able to get to work. This isn't personal; I've told you that already."

Fia nodded, she was too tired to argue. He waited until she'd found her spare key beneath the mat, put it in the lock and opened her door before he drove back to the office, and she was asleep wrapped up under the covers barely a few moments later.

The following morning Fia was so exhausted that her eyeballs felt as though they were going to melt at any moment. She curled her arms up onto the reception desk and rested her head on them for five minutes, until the clock ticked over to nine am and Tony would unlock the main front doors.

"Morning," he said to her as he did so.

Fia felt as though she'd only just blinked. "Good morning, Tony," she replied. "We haven't spoken for a while."

"Yes, well. You're very popular on reception now, so you've not got much time for me – and it's just as well, with the number of clients that lot upstairs are dealing with at the moment." Tony stretched out, his arm muscles popping. "Let's see how many people we get through the doors before we close. Which reminds me of something - do you know what happened to the little one that I found?"

"The boy?" Fia sighed. "There was a meeting the other day. The mother kept saying the father was in the room, but the father could prove he wasn't related to the boy at all. He had a DNA test with him. I don't know what happened after that, but I think the partners are still looking after him. I hope they are, anyway, he shouldn't be where he isn't wanted."

"Hmm. That's a sad state of affairs. He was a cute one. Anyone would be lucky to have him as a kid."

"Do you have children, Tony?"

Tony paused in his pat-down of all his

pockets, and twisted the aerial on his radio until he was happy with it. "My wife and I were not blessed, no."

"That's a shame. A good man with no child, and a good child with no father. Life can be a real lottery, can't it?"

"I think you're half-right there," said Tony, humouring her. "But you aren't listening to the mother. Didn't she say that the father was in the room? She should know, after all. Maybe his father isn't that far away after all."

Fia tried to get her sleep-fogged brain into gear. "What are you saying?"

"Nothing. I'm just repeating what you said to me. It's none of my business. But there must be a reason she chose this law firm. Follow the evidence, isn't that what the lawyers say?"

"Or bury it," murmured Fia.

Tony nodded, and firmly closed his mouth. He was done talking. Fia stifled a yawn and turned the computers on, parking the conversation. She had so much to do; she didn't have time to decipher Tony's conspiracy theories.

"What's got you so tired then?" Louella asked, walking in as fresh as a daisy and ready to start the day. "Late night? Who with – do tell."

Fia sat up straight. "I just didn't sleep well, okay?"

Louella whistled, and flicked on the computer screens. "Defensive," she said. "Definitely the sign of a guilty conscience. You can go and get us both a coffee as your punishment. Off you go."

"Fine." Fia needed a coffee anyway; she knew she would be running on it today. She shouldn't bump into Joel Bard on the way to the kitchen, she'd already checked the records at reception, and knew that he'd checked into the building at three am after dropping her home. He'd still be up in his office, working away.

She was still irritated. They'd ended the night at odds again, just as they always did, but she couldn't deny he'd saved her from the rain. She owed him one, and that annoyed her even more - maybe that was another reason she had ignored his orders, and turned up at work on time this morning. She didn't want to seem weak next to him. She could cope with the workload if he could.

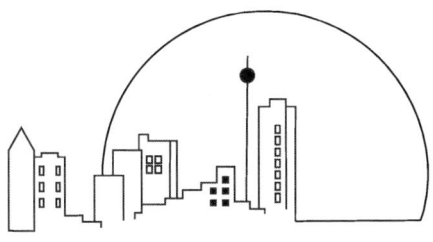

CHAPTER FOURTEEN

The day passed quickly. It was close to closing time when she heard Tony having a conversation with someone at the entrance, and when she looked up there was Joel Bard himself, looking as fresh as an apple covered in dew, hanging daintily from a tree on a spring morning. Fia wondered how on earth he had managed it.

"Mr Bard," Tony said with surprise. "I didn't expect to see you still here."

"Ah, I had a bit of an early start, but then, we're still working on that case for the town council. I can't stand the look of disappointment on their faces when their building regulations aren't delivered on time. Would you mind checking the door for me? It was still sticking a bit when I first came in."

"Of course, Mr Bard." Tony walked away, and Fia was alone with him.

He put a paper bag onto the desk. "Here are your things. Your car keys are in there; I checked."

"You went through my things?" Fia rummaged through it; everything seemed to be present and accounted for. Her handbag was carefully wiped clean from paint, and she made a mental note to thank Susie later.

"What are you checking for? It's all there. I'm many things, but I'm not a thief, so you can put your claws away, woman. I just checked everything was in there, when it was given to me. It's a shame about your car, though."

She went cold. "What happened to my car? Where is it?"

"It's a bad neighbourhood at night, you know that. The man I sent couldn't find it when he got there. I'll have to give you a lift home."

Her heart dropped at the thought of being without transport. Sure, her little Micra was old, but it was the only car she could afford. Her budget at the moment wouldn't run to a bicycle.

"Are you kidding me?" she replied, tearing at the paper of the bag in front of her. "I'll need to go back there, and make a police report- who was it that went to fetch it? Maybe I could talk to them-"

"Of course, I'm kidding you. It's in the work

car park. Oh, and I had it cleaned - it was filthy, be grateful."

"You *were* joking with me?" Fia was incredulous. Joel Bard just hummed and put his hands deep into his suit pockets. "You were trying to make a joke? You failed; that was awful. Don't do that to anyone again, it's not your strength at all."

"Fine, I take the feedback. I suppose I'd better stick to what I'm good at, and so here you go-"

A black box file landed on the desk next to the bag. Fia glanced at it, and then looked up at the smug man in front of her.

"What's this?"

He grinned at her. "Well, I've done you a favour. You owe me one in return. We were trying to keep things equal, weren't we? I need this sorted before court tomorrow."

"What's wrong with it?"

"I dropped it. The pages are numbered, but they're all out of order. I haven't got time to fix it myself. Bring it to my office when you're done, I'll still be here."

Fia flipped open the lid. The box was stuffed with pages; it was going to take hours. Still, if he could work late into the evening, so could she. This was turning into a ridiculous game of chicken.

"Of course, Sir," she kept her reply polite and sweet. "It will be with you as soon as it's done."

"Then... I'll trust you with it," he said.

Fia didn't know what to say. A soft blush prickled on her neck and flew across her collar bones. She wondered if this was the paperwork from his home the night before. Only Joel Bard would apologise for judging her, and then tease her with it at the same time. She picked up the box and motioned hitting him with it. He tutted slightly, but this was the only acknowledgement she got for her moment of rebellion.

On the way to the elevator he nonchalantly reached a hand upwards into the leaves of an orange tree and picked one. The tree rustled slightly and went back to looking perfect. He held it out to her.

"Orange?"

Fia's shoulders shook slightly. "They're ornamental," she said. "You can't eat them."

"Really? Damn. I've been eating these for years now. Do you think I've been poisoned?"

"Probably." Fia took the orange from between his fingers and tossed it into the rubbish bin. He laced his fingers back through hers for a brief moment; she was sure it was accidental.

"Will you care for me, if I'm poisoned?"

"No. You've brought it on yourself. Now let go of me – let go. I have to get back to work, before I'm fired. Have you met the boss here? He's a nightmare."

Joel Bard smiled wryly, and headed towards his office. "Ah; I see you're dreaming of me," he said.

Fia laughed then, and headed to the reception desk, only to see Louella there. Her friend's eyes were huge.

"Tell me you're not fucking the boss," she said.

There was nothing she could say to that. Joel Bard had made it clear that he wasn't interested in any sort of relationship, and anyway, she didn't need the hassle that would come with one as she worked out the end of her contract. She was about to deny it when she realised that she'd taken far too long to respond. Louella sank her head into her hands, and wailed through her fingers.

"Well, that's going to come with a crap-ton of problems. What were you *thinking*? And I had no idea that man could have actual romantic feelings; how did you even manage it? Oh, you poisoned him, didn't you - I heard him say you poisoned him-"

"Lou," Fia interrupted. "Don't worry about it. It's fine. You're misunderstanding. I don't have a single romantic feeling for that man, and he certainly doesn't have any for me."

Her friend hesitated. "Are you lying to me?"

"He's one of the most irritating men I've ever met," Fia told her honestly.

"Fine. I believe you. Even you wouldn't be

that stupid."

"And what's that supposed to mean?" Fia peered into the black box file and winced at the mess of paper inside it.

"Nothing, I'm sure." Louella tapped the lid. "What's this?" she asked. "Did someone leave it here for me?"

"No," she replied. "The CEO gave it to me. He's dropped it, it needs re-ordering. Now you're back I might go and get a head start."

Louella whistled as she looked at it. "Really? He gave this to you?"

"I know, it's really mean!" Fia whined, her tiredness getting the better of her. "He caused the problem, he should fix it himself, right?"

"That's not what I meant. This is high-level clearance, Fia. I've never known any temporary employee get within three feet of one of these boxes. How did you get him to trust you like that?"

"I-"

"It must have been the party," Louella seemed happy with the explanation she'd found for herself. "All your hard work really paid off with that, didn't it? You impressed him with your organisation at the party."

"Maybe?" Fia winced. She reminded herself that her friend didn't know what she'd done at that party. She decided to get away before the conversation continued any further.

"Anyway, he's given it to me, so I'd better get going. I won't be home until midnight at this rate. Why did you suggest this job to me again? You're a terrible friend."

Louella agreed with her, she was a terrible friend. But then to make up for it, she pointed Fia in the direction of an empty boardroom – one with a long table that stretched down the middle of it, with enough chair space to seat thirty people. Once the door was closed the atmosphere seemed muffled; it was sound-proofed. Perfect. Fia would be able to concentrate on the project without any distractions, which would help her sleepy brain.

Fia fanned the papers out across the table, and began to group them in piles of hundreds to begin with. The box was deeper than she first thought, and the piles soon grew tall. She tried not to read them, but certain words kept catching her eye, and she was soon absorbed in it all.

This was evidence for a pro-bono case. The Captain of a boat moored in the harbour had been shot at close range during a robbery. The moorings had come loose as the criminals boarded, and the boat had crashed into its neighbour. The owners of the robbed vessel were suing the Captain they had hired for negligence.

Failure to stop the theft, responsibility for the

damaged hull – they were even complaining about the blood stains that soaked into the oak-lined flooring. The poor man who had been on the boat was still in hospital awaiting another operation to remove fragments of the bullet. Fia placed that information carefully on the fourteenth pile on the table.

One mystery was solved, though. The address linked to the owner of the neighbouring boat was that of a Mr Joel Bard. That explained the suntan, Fia thought. He must spend a lot of time on his yacht with his shirt off. He was such a rich poser. Men like that were a waste of time.

But, still. He wasn't complaining about the damage to his own boat. She couldn't see any compensation claims in the box at all. No, he had simply claimed for the damage on insurance. The owners of the other boat had lapsed insurance, and so they were going after their employee. Not only that, but Joel Bard had agreed to defend the Captain in court for free, despite his crazily busy work schedule. Maybe he was a friend. Perhaps the Captain would talk to him while he sat on the deck, a drink in his hand and the sun shining down on his chest. He'd probably be smiling and happy for once.

Fia had no idea when he would have time for that. She only ever saw him working – but she had seen him relaxed twice now, she remembered. His expression after he'd come, the soft smile as he wiped her lips dry afterwards. She wondered if he had as many versions of himself as she did.

Finally, all the papers were in order and back in the box. Fia looked at the clock, it was almost eleven. She doubted he was still here, but she would go to the office on the seventh floor and see if she could work out why he'd give this job to her and not Louella. To piss her off, certainly. But she wondered if it really was a sign that he trusted her. She decided to stop thinking about it - knowing him, it could just be an opportunity to look like a hero with a boat.

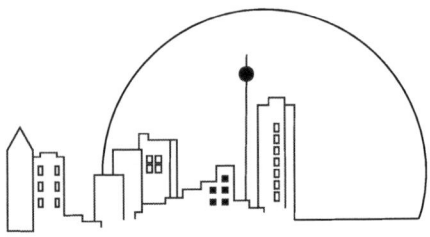

CHAPTER FIFTEEN

The corridors of the law firm at night were completely silent as she walked through them. Just as she was beginning to adjust to the quiet, Fia heard the sound of one single sob, followed by a flurry of tiny breaths inwards. The noise finished before she could tell which room it came from.

She stood dead in the middle of the dark corridor, which suddenly appeared quite spooky, and waited for another one. She began to suspect a ghost. When another high-pitched sob echoed down the darkness of the corridor, Fia began to nudge doors open in a hunt for the cause.

"Hello?" she called. No one answered.

A scurry of movement when she pushed on the next door. Ah, it was this office then. Fia stuck her head around it, and her heart immediately melted. It was the little boy, sitting underneath a table, tears running down his face and mixing with the snot coming out of his nose. She flicked the light on and looked for a box of tissues for him - lawyer's offices always had a supply of tissues as standard; they were forever making someone cry. This box was tucked away on a shelf at the back of the room. She lunged for it, and crouched down by the table.

"Hello little man," she said. "Do you remember me?"

The boy stared at her, his eyes twice the size and reflecting like mirrors; they were full of tears. Before she could think twice about it, Fia hooked her arms beneath his armpits and scooped him onto her lap. He shied away from her as she tried to wipe his face clean.

"Come on now," she said, trying again with a handful of tissues. "Hold still, it's just for a moment."

But the boy was too agitated. He wriggled like a fish, and she gave up for a moment, cursing herself. She was better with children than this. Hadn't she spent lots of time reading to them? She held up the box of tissues. "Do you know what this is? Have you seen one before?"

The boy shook his head, eyes still like saucers.

"This is a tricky box. If you pull one tissue out, another comes into its place, just like magic. Do you want to try?"

He reached out one damp hand and closed it
around the tissue sticking out of the box. Fia smiled at
him with gentle encouragement. He pulled. When
another tissue peeped out of the box, his eyes
widened even further. He pulled at that one. And
another, and another. Fia thought she heard a watery
giggle, but she couldn't quite be sure. They must be
halfway down the box by now. She intercepted him
and took one for herself, dabbing gently at her own
face with it.

"And now we wipe, wipe, wipe," she
instructed. "Nice and clean." The boy copied her
movements, and a long string came away from the
tissue. Fia grabbed another handful and closed her
hand over his. "And Auntie Fia will help you a little
bit, because you need more cleaning than me. Look
at that, all tidy and sorted. Shall we have a look in my
bag and see if I have any sweeties in there?"

He nodded, and Fia was grateful to find a bar
of chocolate hiding at the bottom of her handbag. She
dusted it off and tore the foil for him. While he
devoured it, she returned the pile of belongings she'd
removed in her search, the largest of which was Paul's
book. She hesitated. It was too late to stick it back in
her bag; the boy was already looking over her
shoulder at the colourful pictures.

"Do you like this book?" she asked, her

hands shaking slightly as she raised it up so he could get a better look at the front cover.

"Yes." A quiet breath of a word.

"Do you want me to read it to you?" she asked through her rising nausea.

"Please."

"If you tell me your name I will."

"Michael," the boy said.

The boy shuffled fully onto her lap, and she sat cross-legged to accommodate him. He sucked at the chocolate. She raised the book up so he couldn't touch it with his sticky fingers.

"It's all right," she suddenly heard Paul's voice inside her head. "You know I wouldn't care. This book was written for children, wasn't it?" and suddenly the sickness receded, and the title of the book swam into focus.

"All right then, Michael. Let's find out what happens, shall we? I can't wait." Fia cracked the spine with trembling fingers, and found the first page. The words began to spin; the letters jumped about as she fought to read them.

"Breathe," she heard Paul's voice again. "It's only our practice book, so practice."

Fia took a deep breath, and watched the words grow steady. She began to sound out the letters, and the story soon followed.

"A long time ago, there was a magic sword,

but it got lost – do you see the sparkles on the sword?"

"Pretty."

"Yes. Well, this sword could cut anything..." Fia continued on, and after Michael agreed to have his hands wiped and a small drink of water, she even let him turn the pages. He grew more and more sleepy, and eventually collapsed against her, his eyes closed.

There was a shadow in the doorway. She'd noticed it arrive some time ago but it seemed content to wait there, so she hadn't paid it any mind. Now she could stop reading, and so she closed the book and turned to look at the other member of her audience.

Joel Bard stood in the doorway, one hand on the frame. He was looking at her in a way he never had before, and she didn't recognise the expression. It was as though a thought had just occurred to him, and he couldn't process it. For a man usually so firm in his opinions, it was alien to see it on his face. Fia braved a small smile.

He almost spoke then, but she shushed him, pointing warily to the sleeping child. He simply nodded, and reached forwards to pull the boy out of her arms, and they walked back out into the hallway together.

"Thank you for finding him," he whispered. "He's been missing for over an hour; we've been so worried."

"What's going to happen to him?" Fia asked, all concern. "This just isn't right."

He shrugged, and the boy shifted in his arms. "I'm not running the case, Darby is. I just jumped in to help when I heard he was missing. I think I'll take more of a hands-on interest now - I trust my cousin implicitly but he may have more than he can cope with here."

"Will you let me know what happens to Michael?"

He nodded as a thought occurred to him. "Where did you get that book?" he asked. "The illustrations are very familiar."

She tucked it safely back into her bag. "Oh, this old book? I've had it for a while. Read it a million times."

"It sounded like you have. You know it very well. You're very good at reading; I was surprised."

"Yes, well. I had to be good at something, right?"

He closed his eyes in a pained expression. "I was rude to you when you began to work here. I was... concerned. Darby pushed so hard to get you to join the company, and I wondered at his motives. It was wrong of me. I apologise."

His motives? It took a moment for Fia to understand him. "What kind of woman did you think

I was?" She thought back to their previous encounters, and her stomach screwed up into a ball. "Oh. There were other things you thought I was good at."

"No, I didn't mean..." his face pinched.

"Darby is a family man, everyone says so. He was just helping me to get a job."

"I wasn't trying to imply-" he looked distraught now, but Fia could barely see him through the film of anger and shame.

"You thought I was sleeping with him? I thought you just said you trusted your cousin. Is that why you got closer to me? You only thought I was here for one thing?"

"No. I promise, I stopped thinking about you that way a long time ago."

"I don't believe you!" Fia felt sick.

"Shh, please, you'll wake the child," Joel Bard spoke low under his breath as Fia's voice began to rise.

"The first time I met you, I called you an asshole. In case you were wondering? You are still an asshole. Stay away from me. And the next time I see your car? I'm covering it in mud, I'm not just sitting on it."

"That was you? Are you really stalking me or something?" he spluttered, grabbing her by the shoulder. It hurt. Fia wrenched herself free, and shoved the black box she carried underneath his free arm.

"You spend too long working in this place. Not everyone has an ulterior motive. Grow up."

She turned on her heel and marched away, leaving him alone in the dark corridor. She only glanced back when she reached the fire doors at the end. In the faded light, he and the boy he carried wore the same expression of abandonment. They had the same mirror-eyes, and the same sloped cheekbones as Joel Bard simply stood stock-still in the centre of the hallway. Fia was almost running through the door at this point; he couldn't catch up with her holding the sleeping Michael, and he didn't even try.

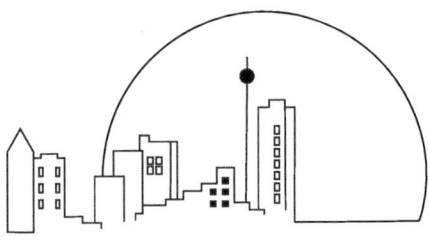

CHAPTER SIXTEEN

There were upsides and downsides to getting to the club so early in the evening. Louella had insisted that they would manage to get a table and be able to catch up properly, and that they could talk before the music was turned up loud, and the crowd began to dance. Fia, in turn, had worried that this gave everyone much more time to drink. Susie was already nervous about enjoying herself for the first time after the death of her boyfriend, and she refused to have an opinion on the matter.

In the end Louella had won, and the three women claimed a corner booth at eight in the evening, next to a wall of neon tubes that gently cascaded through all the colours of the rainbow. Susie was wearing a glittery crochet dress that hugged her all the way down. She told them that she'd made it herself, and it suited her. The flecks of glitter twisted into the yarn bounced tiny squares of rainbow colours over Louella, who wore a tight black military suit. She looked like a sexy model that would crush anyone who offered to fight.

Fia sat down opposite them, arranging her white dress that glowed over the deep suntan she'd got after walking through the sunshine flooded streets of the City all summer. It was lower-cut than she remembered, and the diamond 'F' of the necklace she always wore was visible today, and glittering in the lights.

"I hope you don't mind, but Charly might join us later," said Louella. She continued to explain when she saw the puzzled looks on their faces. "My girlfriend? She said she wanted to dance. I delayed her for a bit so I could catch up with you lovely people. You've met her, Fi. From the shop."

"You're still together?" Fia was surprised.

"Shocked?"

"I've never known you stick with someone for so long. You must be growing as a person," Fia retorted, watching their drinks being made at the bar. It seemed to involve a lot of work, and she wondered what on earth Louella had ordered.

"Yes, well," Louella shifted uncomfortably. "I like her. Actually... she's moved in. And we've got this sort of commitment thing going on."

"Congratulations," said Susie. "What's the commitment? I don't see a ring."

"I don't mean that," Louella screwed up her face. "We've got a dog. Picked her up last week. Cute, but she leaves hair on everything. White hair on a black suit, I probably look horrendous. Love is sacrifice though, am I right?"

Fia examined her closely. She looked as pristine as ever; the suit was immaculate. "Yes, she said. "I see it now, you're a mess."

Louella pretended to be insulted. "Thanks. And actually, we are engaged – have been for ages. There's no need to make such a big deal about it, is there?"

"Congratulations," said Fia, surprise colouring the word. "How long did you wait before proposing? A day?"

Her friend shrugged. "When you know, you know. We're waiting on the rings."

Their faces all changed from pink to green as a waiter put three large glasses down on the table. They also looked green, but this was their actual colour and not a reflection from the neon light.

"What are these?" Fia removed the orange slice, and ran her finger around the sugar rim. She licked it, and regretted the decision.

"That's salt, you idiot." Louella looked highly

amused.

Susie took a sip. "Strong," she commented.

"I thought we could start with something stronger, just to get us relaxed. We can calm down in a bit, no point in going overboard. Just this drink," a waiter put a string of tiny glasses in front of them, "-and a few shots... and then we can behave ourselves," Louella added after taking one look at Fia's face.

"Okay," Fia said, picking up the first shot glass and downing it.

Susie's eyebrows rose. "Have you changed a lot in a year, Fi? I've never known you to be so enthusiastic about drinking."

"I've had a bad week." And she had, avoiding her boss at every turn.

"Do you know what's going on?" Susie turned to Louella.

"No." Louella shuffled some of the shots away from Fia's reach and gave one to Susie. They lightly clinked them together before swallowing them. "I just know her behaviour at work has been off all week, like she says. Skittish, like a kitten trying to balance on a rubber ball. It's a guilty conscience, must be. Give her another shot then ask her what she's been up to."

Susie grinned, and pushed another into Fia's hands. "Do tell," she invited.

"Oh, I get it. This is an ambush, isn't it? Well, I haven't done anything, so you're pointing at the wrong target." Fia drank the shot.

"Then why are you avoiding the boss?"

"You didn't sleep with him, did you?" Susie looked concerned. "You need this job, at least for the moment. That wouldn't be very smart."

Fia choked on her suspicious green drink, which tasted like poison. "If you must know, I'm angry with him. He's an asshole. I told him that, so he knows he is one now. He's an asshole," she instructed Louella, tapping her firmly on the elbow in time to her words. "Don't believe a word he says."

It was obvious the alcohol had hit her bloodstream quickly. Susie called for some water to be brought to the table, while Louella continued to question her bravery.

"You said that to his face - to the face of our miserable CEO - and you haven't been fired? I don't believe it."

So Fia told them about her argument with Joel Bard, and his belief that she was Darby's mistress. She left out all mention of their encounters in the elevator and the kitchen. She had a strong feeling that she knew what her friends would say about that.

"Darby hired you because I asked him to!" Louella was furious. "He should know his cousin better than that!"

"And he doesn't know you at all," soothed Susie. "You wouldn't have sex with your boss, especially not if he's married."

Fia nodded, and tried to look very innocent.

"He should keep his opinions about my friends to himself," Louella fumed. "I can make his life very difficult if I want to. I've only got to start filing things in the wrong places. And to insult Darby like that as well. What an...an..."

"Asshole," supplied Fia helpfully.

"Yeah." she said forcefully, rolling up her sleeves. "Ten out of ten for the diagnosis."

"I'm surprised, though. I thought he was nice. He takes an interest in other people, has an opinion on art... I felt he was kind. We had a lovely conversation, the day he came to my studio. I thought he was a boss that cared about his employees," remarked Susie.

Fia started in shock. "What do you mean, when he came to your studio?"

"To pick up your car. You remember you left it there, right? He drove it back to the office for you. It must have been a bit of a bother for him though; it took me ages to find your keys. We had to ransack the place. You know I'm not that tidy."

Fia tried to imagine Joel Bard changing gear in her rusty Nissan Micra. She couldn't quite manage it. "Did he mention me at all? What did he say?"

Susie weighed up her answer. "Well, we did talk about you a little bit. I mean, it was the only thing we had in common. I don't think I told him too much-" She hesitated. "Wait; do you think that's why he was there? Checking up on you? Oh, I hope I didn't say anything I shouldn't have. Is he really an asshole? He seemed so nice!" Susie looked distraught, but Fia just gave her a small, comforting kick under the table.

"Don't worry about it. I haven't got anything to hide." It was only a half-lie. Fia didn't have anything to hide from Joel Bard, but from Susie herself.

Susie sighed in small relief. "What will you do about it, though? Will you quit? I mean, you have to keep working while you can't write - you need the money. Do you want me to hire you at the studio? It wouldn't be as much, but I could help. At least until you can work at your books again."

Fia looked at her two friends in front of her, and suddenly felt a lot lighter. They looked as angry as she felt, and they were there for her. She suddenly felt incredibly lucky, and the ill-feeling drained away. Today wasn't about being miserable, after all, and she suddenly just wanted to have a great time, and forget about everything.

"I read Paul's book this week," she said. Susie went suddenly still. "I managed to open it, and I read it. The words didn't jump around at all."

"You did?"

162

"Thank you for giving it to me at the painting studio. I don't know if I remembered to say that when you gave it to me, but I am grateful. I'll stay on reception for a bit longer, just while I get myself together, but don't worry. I'll be writing again soon – I can feel it all beginning to come back." This was an exaggeration. Fia wasn't sure she could make the stories form in her head just yet, but she wanted everyone to calm down, and enjoy the night.

Susie gave her a watery smile, and Louella punched the air and whooped. "Then this evening is a celebration," she sang, waving towards the waiter once more.

"And this is my round," replied Fia, singing along in tune.

The evening flowed into night. The time wheeled by as the club grew louder, and the dance beat pulsed through the walls. The place was soon packed. Louella's girlfriend turned up, and she looked Fia's dress up and down before giving her an approving nod, and dragging Louella onto the dance floor.

A guy leaning on the bar kept looking over at their table, then glancing away quickly. Susie giggled.

"There's someone over there who's interested in you," she said.

Fia glanced round. "Nope, you're wrong."

"Am I that bad at this? I know I've been out

of the game for years, but I can still tell when someone is paying attention." Susie actually pouted, and Fia began to count the drinks she'd had in her head before replying.

"He's not looking at me, he's checking you out. Probably wondering how quickly your dress will unravel if you snag it," she said.

Susie was fighting the urge to hide underneath the table. "Really? Don't say things like that. Really? I have no idea what to do."

Fia shrugged. "I'd say just ignore him, but there are two reasons you can't."

"And what are they?"

"One, he's cute, and two – he's coming over to talk to you."

Susie looked back at the bar, which now had a gap in the bodies leaning on it. She looked upwards to see the cute man leaning over the back of the booth, elbows planted into the cushioning of the seating.

"Hello," he said.

Susie glanced fearfully at Fia, who toasted her before drinking.

"It's a dance, or a drink, or both," she said. "Nothing terrible. Nothing wrong. Paul would want you to be happy." She looked at the dance floor, watching Louella and her girlfriend tango across the centre of it. "Go have fun. I need to think about something anyway. If he misbehaves, tell Lou. She'll poison him."

"I think she's already poisoned us," returned Susie, smiling at the guy who was now pointing at the dance floor. Fia couldn't hear what he was saying over the music. "I'll see you later."

The neon lights in the club changed from orange to pale blue, before sinking to a darker purple. This completely matched Fia's mood, which had begun to drop again. The dancers in the club swarmed over the floor, but despite several invitations from her friends she didn't want to join them.

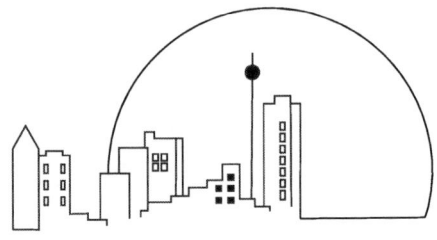

CHAPTER SEVENTEEN

Fia sat alone in the corner booth, sipping at whichever cocktail Louella had considered fashionable this time round, pulling her lips tight with every sip. It was too sweet; bright red and sugary with a blackberry nestled at the bottom of it. She felt like a sugar-addicted vampire. It didn't taste like alcohol at all, and this concerned her; it was probably deadly. Her head was beginning to swim.

Soon she wasn't alone; someone pushed into the booth next to her, jogging her elbow and spilling red down her white dress.

"Sorry," he said. "I'll buy you a new one." She didn't know if he meant the drink or the dress, but she didn't care. "You look beautiful," he shouted in her ear. His cologne was overpowering; a mixture of earth, grapefruit and engine grease. He probably thought it made him manly; Fia couldn't imagine any woman finding it attractive.

"Thanks," she shouted back, looking away from him and wondering if he would just leave. She couldn't get out of the booth unless she climbed over him, or the table. Her ruined dress was too short for either option.

But he grabbed her leg above the knee, giving it a shake to get her attention again. "What would you like to drink?"

"Nothing. I've had enough. I'm going soon, you'd better go and talk to someone else," she shouted over the music.

"Just one- no? Really? That's a shame. You're really hot. Stay for a bit longer?" His eyes roamed every inch of her body, and zeroed in on her cleavage. She felt dirty everywhere that he looked.

"I need to go to the bathroom," was all she said. She stared at him until his eyes fell, and he shuffled back out of the booth. Fia seized the moment and pushed out past him, leaving it empty. It was a shame they'd lose the table, but it was a small price to pay to get rid of Mr Sleaze. She headed for the ladies' room.

Inside she ran cold water over her hands and arms, trying to cool down. The rainy season had lowered the temperature, but it was still warm and the air was now very damp. Most of the dancers had shirts sticking to their backs from the sweat of it, and most women in the bathroom were dabbing at their foreheads with cool tissues. The night was turning into a melting pot of emotions, and the crowd were moving in one mass of heat.

She examined herself in the mirror, wiping the drink stain on her dress before giving it up for lost and looking at her reflection. Icy blue eyes still stared back at her. It was the one feature she really hated about herself; her cold eyes. Her brother had often teased her about them. He said that if she'd ever gone into acting as a career, she would constantly be playing the villain. But she'd never taken his teasing words badly – after all, he had once had the same eyes himself.

"Am I happier?" she whispered. "Do I look happier? Susie does. Is this good?"

A couple of young women came in together, giggling and banging the cubicle doors shut. They gossiped about their dates through the chipboard between them.

"Hey," one called out to her from behind the stall door. "Is there any paper in the one next door? This one's out."

Fia pushed the doors of the others open. "No," she called back. "It's all gone."

"Oh, okay," said the voice again, and she

could hear the girl rummaging through her bag. "I'm out of tissues though – tell me... have you got two fives for a ten?"

Fia just sighed, and left the bathroom. Perhaps it was time to go home. She would go and find the others, and see how they felt about making a move from here.

But the same man waited for her outside the door, smirk in place. He gestured again at the dance floor, and winked at her.

"No," she said, and tried to walk around him. He blocked her way. She wheeled around in the other direction, but he was in front of her again, a clear foot taller than her and twice as wide. This could turn into a problem.

"Be nice," he said, taking a step forward. His body pushed onto hers, knees to chest. He began to dance and grind against her, his muscles a wall that she couldn't escape from. "If you don't want a dance, have a kiss, yeah? You should loosen up a bit - we're all here to have some fun."

His face was too close to her face. His breath was pure alcohol. Suddenly his mouth was on hers, wet and awful. He pushed hard against her lips, and they caught against her teeth. Fia tried to push him away, but he was too big. She managed to get a hand free from his dance hold and hit upwards under his ribs, the way she'd been taught in self-defence classes at university, but he was too drunk to register the pain.

All at once, Fia felt a lot lighter. The iron grip around her was gone, and the man was thrown back, reeling against the restroom door from a punch to the kidneys. Joel Bard stood over him, his mouth set in a familiar thin line of anger.

"Get lost," he said.

Fia stumbled for a moment, but then her boss was there, taking her gently by the elbow and leaning her against the barrier that separated the dance floor from the rest of the club.

"Are you okay? Do you need anything?"

She was trying not to be too confused; the alcohol was really settling in now. "I punched him. I tried," she said.

"I know you did."

"You were better at it than me."

"I don't think so. I just got his attention first. He's too drunk to feel it now, but he'll hurt where you punched him tomorrow. Well done. Do you want me to find him, so you can do it again?"

Fia shook her head no. She just wanted to go home now. It had been an interesting night, when all was considered. "Why are you here – are you stalking me, now?"

"I'm out with some clients. It's not too much of a coincidence. Grow up." His lips twitched.

"Touché," she said with feeling.

"You don't need to say that to me."

"Then I'll say thank you."

He waved her thanks away as though it was an irritating fly. "Don't mention it."

Fia suddenly remembered her conversation earlier. "Susie said you collected my car for me yourself. You didn't need to do that - I was happy to pick it up after work. You had an emergency that day."

He shrugged. "That's okay. I found I had some spare time. My driver dropped me off, it was no trouble."

"I didn't want-"

"Me driving your car? I treated it well. I had one similar myself, when I was a student. What?" He saw the expression on her face and started to laugh. "You can't imagine that? I'm not as stuck up as you think I am."

"I don't know whether you're stuck up or not. I don't judge people before I know them," Fia snapped. It came out more sharply than she had intended.

"Touché," was his only reply. She remained leaning against the barrier, looking out into the sea of colour-changing bodies. She could see Susie laughing, and Louella resting her head onto her girlfriend's shoulder. Joel Bard leaned next to her. He said nothing, and for a minute she just breathed, and enjoyed the company.

Fia soon noticed flickers of attention in their direction, her friends darting looks at her. She realised that his white shirt and her white dress were glowing brightly over the crowd, changing colour in unison, a beacon across the room.

"I'm going outside," she said abruptly, heading for the exit. "I need some water and fresh air."

"Are you alright?"

"I can still taste him in my mouth. I don't like it."

"I'll get you the water," he said, ignoring her protestations. "Don't argue; I'm coming with you. We have no idea whether that man is still out there. I almost hope he is. Fucker."

She'd never heard him swear before. She didn't know how to argue with this new version of her CEO, and so Fia allowed herself to be manoeuvred through the crowd, and she was soon sitting on a low wall outside the club. The air was only slightly cooler out here; oppressive clouds hung heavy in the dark sky, and she knew it was lucky it wasn't raining.

At least they were away from the prying eyes of her friends. She was grateful that they couldn't see her with Joel Bard, because that would lead to several questions that she didn't have a clue how to answer.

The man in question sat beside her and handed her a plastic cup of water. Fia sipped at it as a slight breeze whipped around the corner of the building, freezing the sweat on her body and making her shiver slightly despite the heat.

He put his arm around her and pulled her close as she finished drinking the water.

"Better?"

"Yes. Thank you, Sir," she said. She couldn't seem to help teasing him. That last cocktail had created a strange bravery inside her, and dulled her worry about consequences.

He looked at her strangely then, and seemed to be making his mind up about something. His fingers gripped at her waist, and then relaxed again. She looked up at him questioningly.

"You have nice eyes," he murmured. "Bright, like the sky several stories up."

She continued to stare at him, bemused by the idea of poetry being said to her on the wall in the middle of the night, until she saw him mouth the words 'damn it' under his breath as he pulled her tighter to him.

"I'll take the taste of him away for you," he said, and licked his way into her mouth. It was messy, and unthinking. Fia found herself returning the kiss with the same amount of violence, swallowing his saliva and forgetting to breathe. It wasn't long before they were forced to stop for air, both of them panting, both of them shaken.

He laughed as his hands wound through her hair, tipping her slightly, bringing her mouth into line with his. He pulled back slightly and brushed their lips together, forwards and backwards in a gentle whisper before looking into Fia's eyes for permission. She stuck the tip of her tongue out at him in response, and when he did the same she sucked gently at the tip of it. His body shuddered.

"Shit," he said. "What the hell am I doing, I-"

She pressed her lips against his to stop him talking, and he kissed her thoroughly before gently holding her lower lip between his teeth and pulling. It stung.

"Naughty," he said.

Fia dipped her head, and pretended to care, pretended to be shamefaced. She was instantly distracted. His body was a film of sweat; the air was growing heavier by the second. The dampness made his shirt cling to him, see-through and wet. She could count the hair on his chest, she could see the peaks of his nipples through the thin cotton, and she wanted to twist them, to make him jump. She brushed over one experimentally, but he caught at her hand at once.

"Very naughty. What am I going to do with you? This is a bit too public-"

They were kissing again, and she didn't know

who had started it this time. He tasted of whiskey; it was obviously a favourite drink of his, it was becoming familiar to associate it with him. She heard a faint moan from the back of his throat, a whisper of profanity. She wasn't sure where he ended and she began any more, they were so close. There was a single burst of lightning across the sky, followed by a voice that made them stop instantly.

"Fia! Where are you? We're going home!" It was Louella.

Fia put one trembling hand on his chest and pushed him away. "Go."

"But-"

"My friends are here. I'm safe. Go."

He seemed torn. "I do need to find my clients – I'm being a terrible host."

"It's fine, they'll be here any minute-"

A rumble of thunder. Louella's voice followed it. "Fia! Let's get home before the storm, yeah? The queue for a taxi is going to be a mile long already."

Fia saw them then, waving at her from the doorway of the club. She looked for Joel Bard, but he was gone. She stood up from the wall and brushed brick dust from her behind. This dress would be going in the bin when she got home.

"Here I am," she said. "Let's go."

Louella grinned. "Let's," she said. "Oh, I was going to ask you; did you see Mr Bard? I'm sure it was him. Did you see him, Susie? There was a guy here that looked just like our CEO."

Fia tutted. "You've been working too much overtime, Lou. You're beginning to see work everywhere you go. Maybe it's time to take a vacation."

Louella laughed, and threw an arm over her shoulder. "Let's find a taxi. We've only got about twenty minutes until the heavens open."

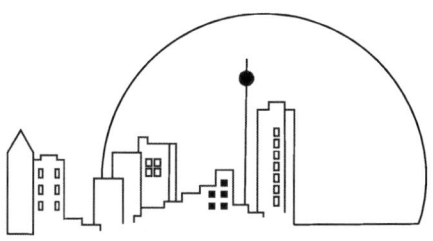

CHAPTER EIGHTEEN

The morning came, and a glimpse of sunshine followed the storm from the night before. The heavy rain had wiped the dust and grime of the summer away from the streets, and they were gleaming in the rays of it; washed clean and ready to start a new season. Fia stood on the high cliff to one side of the financial district and looked down at it all, holding one end of a designer dog lead. The other end was clipped onto the latest addition to Louella's family, which was currently sniffing at a bush with interest. The dog had friendly eyes that shone like black beads, and beautiful white-and-copper fluffy hair that would be soaked in mud in no time at all.

Fia had no idea what breed it was, animals were not her forte, but it was the perfect size; just small enough to pick up and manoeuvre, but large enough not to shiver constantly like a miniature earthquake. It padded over the ground delicately, barely tugging at the lead, a picture of politeness. She wouldn't have expected anything else from Louella's pet.

Her owners were away at a family wedding, and Fia had agreed to care for it for the day. The poor thing would be bored alone at home, and it was an excuse for her to walk off the ravages of her hangover from the night before. She could feel her headache beginning to lift as soon as she left the smog of the traffic and headed for the small valley nestled on the other side of the cliffs, which was now the City reservoir. Once it had been a small village, but as the high rises expanded and the City grew, the government had flooded the valley to supply water to all the homes that were needed for the migrating workers.

A gravel path wound its way around the edges of it, and trees and bushes dipped low over the deep, still body of water in the middle. Fia didn't know how deep it was, but it was enough to drown the tall spire of the village church that stood in the centre of the valley. She picked up a small handful of the stones from the path, and threw them into the lake one by one as she walked. They disappeared into the depths with barely a sound, disturbing the flowing pattern of fish that swam there. Some were multi-coloured goldfish, unwanted pets that had been dropped into the water and continued to thrive. Fia imagined turning on the tap at home, and a tiny fish coming out with her tap water.

The dog sat back and scratched at its neck, pulling at its collar and making the tags on it chime together. Fia took the opportunity to pause and gaze across the water, at the birds swimming and the children learning to kayak on the far banks.

Yes, this was the closest thing to a gentle countryside walk that the City knew. Fia felt her stomach settle, and her head clear. Her hangover may have finally left her, but her embarrassment remained, and her insides clenched every time she thought about the end to the evening. She should never have kissed him - not now she knew he was the CEO of the company, not since she'd found out what he really thought of her. Her cheeks heated up when she thought of his hands on her the night before, the way he looked at her, the expression on his face when he searched her blue eyes with his grey ones. They'd both been drinking, and that was all there was to it.

But then, it was difficult to know how drunk Joel Bard had been last night; his expressions were always so still, and his face didn't show much expression - it was pulled too high over his cheekbones. It was only his large eyes above them that gave him away. Come to think of it, he was very much like the little boy Michael. Fia thought of them both together in the hallway on the seventh floor: they had identical looks of concentration, and similar smiles when they got something they wanted.

She could almost see his face reflected in the ripples of the water. The way his eyes lit up when he saw her; the animation in his usual frozen features when he caught sight of her unexpectedly when they were at work. She'd pretended not to notice it for too long, but she knew. He looked at her with the same expectation that Michael had looked at Paul's book, when she'd read it to him. She was a promise of entertainment. Just entertainment, not love.

The dog pulled gently at the lead and whined, and she began to trudge through the wet gravel of the path once more - but it was soon obvious that the animal wasn't interested in the walk, but wanted to go to the edges of the reservoir. It twisted towards the bank, feet scrabbling in the dirt as it tried to climb down the banks of the muddy shoreline, and as it whined again, Fia thought she heard an answering echo bounce from the surface of the water.

Then she saw that a kayak had broken loose from the pack on the other side of the lake, and was drifting slowly towards them. It was almost too far away to make out the occupant, but as it drew closer she could see a young girl sitting inside it, waving her arms and crying. She didn't appear to be holding a paddle.

Louella's beloved dog gave a series of barks and pulled sharply on the lead. Fia slid through the gravel and mud beside the pathway, and dropped her end of it. A tiny splash followed, and she watched the naughty puppy swim away from her through the water, heading towards the distressed girl, muddy water soaking through its white coat and staining it brown. Louella was going to kill her, but there was no time to worry about it now; the girl seemed to be in trouble, and she and the dog were completely unreachable. Fia wanted to call out after it, but she realised that she had no idea what name it answered to; she'd forgotten to check, and Louella had always called her 'my baby'. With no desire at all to call that out in public, Fia contented herself with cries of "Here, girl!" and "Treats! Come and get a treat!"

She clambered down the muddy bank, and paddled through the rocky shallows of the reservoir, the sharp edges of them biting at her through the soles of her thin sneakers, keeping an eye all the while on both the tiny shape of the puppy, which was swimming hard, and thankfully not showing any signs of tiring yet, and also the kayak itself. The girl had stopped crying now, her mouth an O of surprise as she saw the disobedient fluff-ball coming towards her, and she was still slowly drifting closer and closer.

Soon the dog was scrabbling at the plastic of the tiny boat, and the girl reached down and scooped it into her arms.

Fia breathed out all the air that she didn't realise she was holding. "Hey!" she cried out, waving both hands over her head, and she saw an answering wave from the girl.

She realised that there was no current in the artificially created lake, and so it must be the strong wind that pushed her across it. Fia looked up at the direction that the clouds were moving in, and realised that the breeze would push the little sailors away to the left of her, and they wouldn't make it to the shore. She began to hunt around the bank for a long stick buried in the piles of leaves around her, and eventually found a stout branch that wasn't too rotten from the heavy rains, and which probably wouldn't break if she pulled on it.

Wading out to her waist, she felt the cold water soak through her jeans, and her legs became heavier and heavier to move as she pushed one in front of the other. She held out the branch as far as it could go, the muscles in her arms complaining at the weight of it. The girl had snuggled the puppy down between her knees, and she reached for the free end which danced about over the waves, finally snagging it as she swept past. There was a violent tug on the end of the branch - it was almost too heavy for Fia to hold onto - she had almost let it go when she registered a splashing next to her, and a second pair of hands grasped onto the branch above hers. They pulled the kayak in together, arm over arm, until they could catch onto it and tug it to shore.

Once they were all safely back on shore, Fia tied the ill-fated kayak carefully to a tree that overhung the lake, and turned to greet her fellow-rescuer. The other woman was now cradling the little girl in her arms, and Fia realised that the little sailor was much younger than she'd first supposed. The puppy danced around their legs, jumping up to place her paws on their knees, and licking at the feet of the rescued child.

"There, you're safe now. I told you that you were too young to try paddling by yourself," said the woman in frustration. "I'm going to have such words with your father when we get home, and you can forget about trying this again until you've grown up a bit, understand?" The child didn't answer her; she was too busy reaching down towards the puppy. "Fine," her mother put her down. "You can say thank you to the nice little doggie, while I say thank you to her owner, but then we're going back to dry you off, okay?"

"Oh, I'm not her owner," Fia began to say, but she didn't manage to finish the sentence before the other woman was taking her hand and shaking it, and thanking her for the rescue.

"There are no words I can say; you can't imagine the panic I was in - children, I tell you – do you have kids? No? Well, you'll never be able to imagine the concern of a parent, the worry you have when your own flesh and blood goes missing. Awful, just awful. All you can do is keep looking until you find them, and I'm so very grateful for your help. I won't be sleeping tonight; I can tell you that."

"You're welcome," began Fia, but the woman was already running on over the top of her.

"- And that's it for the playing, young lady. Say goodbye to the doggie, and we'll get you out of those wet clothes as soon as possible."

"Come here, girl," Fia called, reaching for the puppy's collar, but the little animal's perfect behaviour had flown away in the winds, and she hid behind the girl's feet, and growled. She snatched her hand back at once.

"Oh, bless the sweet thing, she doesn't want to leave my baby," said the mother, but her smile didn't quite reach her eyes. "Never mind, hopefully you can bring it to the parkland here another day, and we'll see you then to play. Until then, up you come, angel, and we're on our way, say goodbye – and thank you again, I couldn't rest until I had her in my arms. It was horrendous, watching her stuck in the middle of the lake."

And with that, she nodded, and began to hurry up the pathway, dripping muddy water all the way. Fia looked down at herself and the puppy; they were in no better state.

She cursed herself when she realised that the rescue and the thought of the next few hours scrubbing the dog clean before she returned her to Louella still wasn't enough to turn her mind from thoughts of Joel Bard. The little girl had clung to her mother as she walked away, in exactly the same way the sleeping Michael had subconsciously held on to the CEO.

He'd hunted all through the high-rise for the boy, with the same expression on his face.

Then the sun disappeared behind the clouds as a sudden realisation dawned on her. What had Tony said? That Michael's father couldn't be far away, and there was a reason the divorcing couple used their law firm. Suddenly her sickness returned, and all Fia could taste was the whiskey from his mouth the night before, mixed with the sugar of the cocktails she'd drunk. The back of her throat burned.

She remembered the conversation between the partners, when she hid beneath the orange tree. Joel Bard had refused to give up the boy, he wanted him for himself – and what other possible reason could there be than he was the father?

Everyone commented on the difference

between the two cousins; Darby Bard, the family man, with his two beautiful daughters. Joel Bard, the man who went through life alone, cutting off all the associations that didn't serve him, his private life firmly hidden in the dark. Was Michael his secret? If so, he'd ignored the boy for years, and was leaving him alone when he most needed to step up, and be his father.

The unlikely germ of this idea crawled up her spine, and took root in her head. It bothered her when she returned the puppy to a cooing Louella, and it bothered her when she went to work the following week. She wanted to look Joel Bard in the face again, to examine his features for any sign of the child's - to complete a checklist of his chin, his ears and nose. She didn't know whether she wanted proof that she was right, or that she was wrong. But she was disappointed; he didn't make an appearance all week.

"He's away," said Louella when she asked. "He had a large group of clients arrive last Monday; didn't you hear? He's entertaining them."

"What about the little boy, Michael?"

"Darby's case? I'm not sure. Once they'd found him hiding the other day, they took him to social services. No one could persuade his mother to take him back with her. I can't understand why they didn't do that sooner."

"Oh." Fia compared the boy's fate to that of

her boss, most likely spending the week drinking expensive champagne in golf clubs and partying late into the night. Perhaps he'd had to stay at a hotel. There were probably women in the group, well-groomed and beautiful. He was probably having a wonderful time. She stabbed at a bundle of paper with the staple gun.

"Poor little boy," she said.

"Why are you asking after them?" Louella asked.

"No reason," replied Fia. "How is the puppy? Can she sit still yet?"

Louella was immediately distracted. Fia scrolled through picture after picture of her little fluffy bundle of joy - fetching a stick, folded over with feet in the air, huddled under the duvet between the feet of her owners. Her friend had become surprisingly maternal, and it made her heart glad to see it.

Still, Fia worried over the matter, and one morning, when she'd woken up in bed before the sun rose with the question still bouncing around inside her brain, she decided to go and look for proof herself.

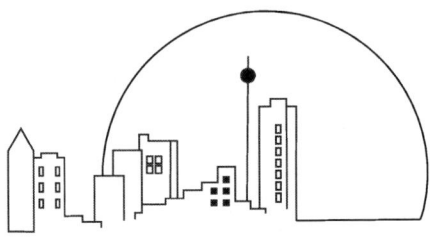

CHAPTER NINETEEN

Fia had never turned up to work so early. It seemed strange to walk through the offices when they were completely empty, and her footsteps echoed over the high ceiling of the atrium. Tony wasn't yet guarding the entrance, it was too early for him, and so Fia met the night shift employee, a woman named Nina. Once Fia showed her ID she didn't have any trouble getting in at that time at all.

"People show up at all times of the day and night here," Nina assured her. "And no one works as hard as the boss. I think he lives here sometimes. It's been weird having him away for so long."

"Does he normally take a week off?" Fia asked nonchalantly. She didn't care, she didn't.

"I've never known it before. Anyway, I'm

sorry you've been dragged into the unhealthy working hours here. Try not to come in too often."

Fia assured her that she wouldn't, and made her way to the seventh floor. She travelled up in the central elevator, just to see if her heart remained on the mirrored wall of it. It did; the cleaners hadn't wiped it clear. They must be a complete bunch of romantics. She traced the outline of it with one fingernail - times had changed since she'd drawn it on in a crisis of confidence. She'd never thought she'd be brave enough to go into Joel Bard's office alone.

There was no lock on his office door. Fia pushed it open slowly with a slight wince. Nina had assured her he wasn't inside, but she couldn't imagine him not sitting at his high-backed chair, starched shirt, rumpled hair where he'd rubbed at it while solving a difficult point of argument. Once inside the empty room she moved quickly. The sky was growing light now, and she wouldn't have long.

The desk drawers were locked, but she ruffled through all the papers on the desk, and opened every box file on the shelves. She was looking for correspondence, photographs, even a stuffed bear or anything that could prove he had a child.

"What am I doing?" she muttered to herself. "This isn't right... maybe I could just ask him..."

It should be all right, as long as she worked quickly. He'd never know that she was in here, and it wasn't as if he'd cared about her privacy, not when he'd gone to see Susie to question her for information, at her art gallery on the outskirts of town. Although that was out in the open, she didn't think that made him more honourable than her – he just didn't care if she found out.

Fia looked at the mess she was creating, while being no closer to an answer. There wasn't anything in the documents that she'd found, only client information, nothing personal. It was time to stop, to put it all back exactly as she found it, to make sure that he never knew she'd been in here. She would have to try and prove her theory another way.

Then, just as she started returning the first folder back to its home, her attention was caught by a picture hanging on the wall. Clouds. Clouds in white, pink and an unpredictable green. All of them had a silver lining. Paul's clouds. It was one of his later works, after he'd had his diagnosis. All his later clouds had a silver lining.

"For others to see," he'd said. "So that they know it's always there."

Tears started in Fia's eyes. She stopped her ransacking immediately, deciding instead to closely examine the brushstrokes, the angled signature in the corner. The personalities of every cloud. She'd never worked out how he did that. She was so absorbed in it that she didn't notice the door opening behind her.

"Do you like it?" said Joel Bard.

Fia froze. "You're back," she said in surprise. "What are you doing here?"

"I might ask you the same thing," he said wryly.

Fia cast about her for an answer, anything she could say that he'd believe. "I'm here to see you," she said.

"Then I'm pleased to see you," he replied simply. And he must be; he looked happy, and he wasn't questioning the early time of day at all.

He's sure of himself, she thought. Of course, he thinks I'm here for him. A wave of anger went through her when she thought of her brother's work hanging in this environment, his optimism mixed up with this man.

"Did you get home all right, last time?" he asked.

"I did," she managed to reply.

"I'm glad." He came into the office properly then; hanging his jacket on the chair and rolling up his sleeves. He tugged at his tie to loosen it, and Fia wanted to remove it for him and strangle him with it. "The streets around here just aren't as safe as they used to be. Car thefts and common assaults have skyrocketed in the last few years – I see them all in court."

Fia nodded, but he waited for a response, so

she worked to fill the silence. She felt awkward, caught in the act.

"How was your week away?" she asked at last.

"Long. They liked to party, and I couldn't keep up with them. I wonder if I am quite antisocial. I'm told I don't often behave well with others." His voice grew quiet, he was forcing the words out now. "Speaking of which, I wanted to apologise. I mean, I wanted to say – about the other night – you'd been drinking, and I shouldn't have – well, we'd both been drinking..."

Fia cut his stumbling words short. She couldn't bear to talk about it. She pointed to the picture on the wall.

"Where did you get that?" she asked.

"Oh," his face brightened. "I bought it recently."

"Where from?"

"From the art studio, when I picked up your car. Do you recognise it? It's an original Paul Devlin. Such a strange place to find one. Do you know the artist?"

"I knew him, yes," Fia corrected, but Joel Bard didn't seem to notice the difference in her words.

"I was so surprised to see it there - I'm a big fan of his. I made the woman who works there an offer she couldn't turn down, although she tried at first. I think she needed the money. She took it down from the wall the second I doubled my price, and hung one of her own pictures up instead. She's very talented in her own right, of course, but I'm glad I got my hands on this one. These paintings are only going to go up in value now; he died last year, did you know?"

"I knew," whispered Fia, completely overwhelmed.

"I particularly like his clouds. I've never seen anyone with his ability to capture light."

That was true, she thought. He lit up any room he walked into. The tears were beginning to sting again.

"I like his sunrises," she managed.

"Me too. Imagine us having something in common. Here-" he spun her around then, away from the picture and out towards the window. "That's why I put my office here."

The sun was just peeping up now. The fiery red ball of it was reflected hundreds of times over in all the windows of the buildings opposite. Soon all the squares of glass shone gold as the sky blushed orange, chasing away the dark. It was a sunrise fit for a man who didn't like being high up in the sky; a replay on a thousand screens just for him.

He was still behind her, and his arms only hesitated for a moment until they crept around her waist, his breath in her hair. Her body responded, he felt so good, but it only took a moment for her brain to catch up with her. She broke away from him.

"Sorry," he said uncertainly.

Fia tore her eyes away from the view in front of her, and looked for the exit. She felt all turned round in such a short space of time. Joel Bard also looked around then, and his eyes widened as he took in the rifled documents, and the files that were pulled from the shelving.

"Are you," his words faltered, "are you going through my stuff?"

"I dropped something. I was just looking for it." It was a stupid lie; she didn't know why she even said it. She felt stupid. Even the clouds in the picture were mocking her. "I have to go."

He studied her, his face evaluating, and as the windows in the distance faded back to their pools of black his expression darkened to match them.

"What do you want?" he asked her evenly.

"I don't know." And she didn't anymore. She couldn't make the situation out at all. "I have to go, I'm sorry." With that, Fia tore open the door to his office and all but ran back down to reception.

It wasn't long before Fia felt the consequences of her actions. Any messages from the Partners now only went to Louella, and her own workload dropped considerably. She was no longer trusted to work on major cases, and if she even made the coffee then Louella would have to carry it to the boardroom.

"What's going on?" her friend demanded some time later. "It's been weeks, I can't keep up with all of this. What did you do to deserve this, Fia?"

But Fia just shook her head, unable to answer, because she couldn't make it out either. It was obvious Joel Bard hadn't told anyone she had ransacked his office, because she still had her job. She couldn't understand why he hadn't used the excuse to terminate her, like he'd wanted to do when she'd first met him. But he hadn't, and instead she had to watch her friend struggle on with the workload alone, and try to find as many little ways to help as she could.

This wasn't a situation that could continue forever. Fia felt worse and worse when she dressed in the morning; her heart sank like a stone when she approached the high-rise owned by the Darby cousins. And of course, it didn't continue. It all came to a head when she was called into the board room four days later.

"It's bad," Louella told her, wringing her hands at reception. Fia had never seen her look so helpless.

"What is?"

"Someone's stealing money from the company. There's a lot gone. You've been named-"

"I'm sorry?"

"There's a lot of money missing. Hundreds of thousands. They've traced it back to you."

She sat down quickly on the chair that was offered to her. "I don't understand."

"Fia," said Louella hesitantly, "Your name is on all the documents."

"What?" This sounded insane. "I didn't do it."

"I know that," said Louella in desperation. "Of course, I know that. I've known *you* since you were six, do I have to remind you of that all the time? If I wasn't aware of what you were capable of by now, I'd be a ridiculous friend. You couldn't plan this and keep it a secret from me in a million years."

"Well, who wrote my name on them?"

"It's not just your name – it's your signature. Someone's obviously got hold of a copy of it, and attached it to everything. Who did you give it to, Fia?"

Fia shrugged, the shock of it all clouding her brain to the point that trying to find any thought was like digging through cotton wool. "What do I do?"

"Heaven knows. I'll help where I can."

Fia had no choice. She didn't bother logging into the computer. She went to the boardroom as instructed, feet like lead, breath thready and high like a drowning butterfly. There were only two other people in it, the two Partners, the same arrangement as her interview.

Darby was conciliatory, but firm. His smile was a little forced, but he offered her one anyway, and Fia realised she would get through this conversation.

"Please take a seat, Fia," he said. "This won't take long."

"I'll stand," she said. Joel Bard seemed frozen in his own chair, and he wouldn't look up at her at all.

Darby nodded. "I'm disappointed in you, Fia. I championed you myself. Joel and I were considering taking you on permanently the other day. I know you only had a contract with us for a year, but we expected more loyalty."

Joel Bard glanced up briefly at the word loyalty. A lump caught in the back of Fia's throat.

"Don't worry," Darby continued, "We won't hold Louella accountable for your actions. I know she only meant well when she recommended you to our company. But you, pending an investigation – we must let you go. Surely you must understand."

This was her moment to defend herself, but Fia struggled to make a sentence. It was all so sudden. "I've never had one thought about stealing from you. I've never had the opportunity," she said.

"You've been caught at least once in places you shouldn't be," Joel Bard spoke then. His voice was low, implacable. "You've found your way into areas that were never meant for you. Your attitude never fit a receptionist, and I believe you capable of crossing any boundaries."

"That's not..."

"Why did you do it?" asked Darby. "If you needed money, could you not have just told us about your problems? Are we not approachable?"

Joel Bard looked anything but approachable. He looked as though one stray spark would catch him alight into a wall of fire.

"I didn't do it," said Fia. "Where is the proof? I want to see it."

"You will," Joel Bard said something at last. "But let me be perfectly clear - you're fired. Get out of the building. We're talking to the police this afternoon."

"I don't think we need to involve the police at the moment," Darby reassured her, a picture of condescension. "We can give you time to return the money. Although we're shocked at your behaviour you were still one of the team, and I believe you must have a conscience hidden inside you *somewhere.*"

Joel Bard hesitated. He looked at her, scanning her eyes, looking for an answer to some mysterious question.

"I didn't do it," she whispered.

"No criminal record," he replied. "I agree with Darby. We won't call the police." His face was in shadow, his hands were fists on the desk in front of him. "I'll give you a chance to change your behaviour, although I doubt it's possible. You'll be all right if you return the money."

He wasn't going to believe her; there was nothing she could do. Darby pressed a button on the intercom system, and Tony was there. He took her lanyard, her security pass. She'd forgotten how big he could look, how threatening if he wasn't on your side. He gestured her out – out of the room, the reception, the building. Louella watched her go.

Not three minutes later, Fia was standing on the concrete outside the offices, the glass doors shut behind her. She stood there until her high heels began to burn her feet, and then she went home.

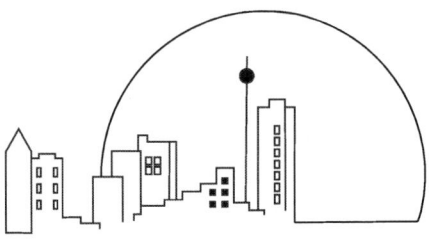

CHAPTER TWENTY

Rage was a stimulating emotion. Over the next few days, Fia didn't leave her apartment; she was either nestled in bed sleeping off her despair, or full of an angry energy that just wouldn't go. She had no routine at all, and once she'd finally dragged herself out of the house and filled her fridge with enough food for a week she found her days were empty again, and her mind wandered everywhere.

Her rooms had never been so clean. She washed the curtains, and scrubbed the sink. She packed all her work clothes away delicately, unable to see them hanging in her room. The mermaid dress shone as she slipped it into a plastic bag and put it under her bed. The memories of that one night were particularly painful.

Fia unfolded all her old clothes and hung them up; the snuggly hoodies and the yoga pants. She dressed comfortably, she allowed herself to breathe. Sometimes the phone rang, but she never answered it.

One late evening she clicked on the angle-poised lamp that sat on her work desk, and it illuminated all the dust that had covered it for so long. This was the last dirty place, the area she hadn't been back to since her brother died.

"I'll just clean it," she whispered to herself. "Nothing more." She ran a damp cloth slowly over the wood of it, revealing the grain underneath. The dust rolled off in one long curl. Once the desk itself was clean, her computer and notepads looked filthy by comparison. She picked everything up and wiped it down, replacing them back one by one. As the clock ticked over to midnight she turned the computer on, pressed a few keys experimentally and then started writing.

Her agent was thrilled to hear it. "Amazing!" she trilled down the telephone. "Are you feeling better? I wanted to give you plenty of space, but...."

"I've started a new book, a new idea," said Fia. "It's a slightly different world. I don't know if it will have a very happy ending."

"Hmm." Her agent considered this politely, but Fia could tell she hated it. "It might be worth finding one. The children do love a happy ending –

but regardless, I can't wait to read it. Are you feeling up for a reading tour? I'm still getting requests from schools across the country. Do you have time?"

"That's the one thing I have a lot of," Fia answered honestly.

"Great. I'll sort some dates. And of course, I hate to ask, but do you have any ideas about an illustrator? We're happy to match you with someone at the company. Anyone would be happy to work with you, I promise."

"But my reputation-"

"The people that know you would never think you were like that, Fia."

"I want someone I can trust."

"Understandable. You don't have to decide now."

"Okay." Fia suddenly thought about Susie, and her delicate brush strokes, her sense of humour. She remembered Joel Bard's admiration of her artwork, and an idea came to her. "I want to talk to someone first," she said. "Someone I could work with."

This was fine, said her agent. She looked forward to hearing more; Fia knew that her door was always open. The conversation lost its drive, and Fia made her excuses, planning to speak to Susie while the ideas were still bright and fresh in her mind.

She tried to ignore another thought – that she

still trusted Joel Bard's judgement, and was allowing it to influence her thinking. He still sat there inside her brain, offering suggestions even though she could never see him again. And he would no longer listen to her. Stay there in my head then, she thought sourly. Make friends with Imaginary-Paul. One day I'll stop listening to the pair of you.

With her book idea still knocking around inside her head, Fia sat on the windowsill in her apartment the following morning with a cup of tea, and watched the rush hour traffic. She waited for it to die down, and then she took her chance to find her way back to the outskirts of town, and to Susie's art studio.

Her car looked exactly the same. She didn't know why she thought it might look different after Joel Bard drove it, but it didn't. There were no extra receipts shoved in her cup dispenser, the seat and mirrors were exactly as she had left them. She thought she smelled a hint of cinnamon from the seat fabric, but it was probably just her imagination. It didn't help that she could never imagine him in this setting - he was from a world of polished leather seats, hand stitched by experts, and she knew he would never be caught dead in a pair of dungarees.

No, the car looked as it ever did, but when Fia walked into the art studio she saw a familiar memory from the past few weeks. It was the middle of the morning art therapy session, and the room buzzed with young voices. She looked over to the far side of the room, and was surprised to see the little boy Michael hand painting alone in a corner. When he saw Fia he trotted over to give her a big hug around her knees.

"Hello, Michael," she said, patting him on the head.

"Why don't you show Fia what you've been painting?" said Susie, walking over to them. Michael nodded solemnly, and went back to his table, pointing at a snarl of paint on the paper there.

"Beautiful," said Fia. "I can't wait to see it when it's finished."

The boy nodded again, and stuck his hand back into the blue, sweeping it across the top of the paper, where it slowly sank into the table as a thick, wet sky.

"Why is he here?" asked Fia.

"I have a contract with the council around here. He's here for therapy sessions – his foster parents dropped him by this morning. It's so sad."

"Yes." Fia tried to figure out if he was painting a rocket ship, or a frog. It was hard to tell.

"They're still trying to find his biological father, but his mother is keeping her mouth tightly closed over it. She's refusing to tell social services anything."

"She said something at work. She said the father was in the room with her," said Fia. "I think it's our CEO." She whispered the last words of the sentence; it was the first time she'd voiced the fear out loud.

But Susie was less than impressed with this idea. "The one I met here? Are you sure? I didn't get that vibe from him at all. That's a man who holds onto something tightly once he's got it, I can tell you that. There's no way he would abandon a child."

"But they look so alike."

Susie stared at Michael, who dipped both hands up to the wrist in red paint, and then slowly rubbed his palms together. She frowned as she studied him.

"Yes, I can see the resemblance," she said. "This little one is a lot more fun, though. You can clean that mess up later, since you know him."

"I'm being serious."

"So am I. Do you have any evidence?"

Fia thought about rifling through Joel Bard's office, her invasion of his space. Then she saw the unguarded expression on his face, his happiness when he saw her. She felt dirty. "No," she said.

Susie shrugged, as though that was the end of the matter. She gave Fia a handful of pencils to sharpen, saying that she might as well be useful if she was going to hang about.

"I do know one thing for sure," she said.

"What's that?"

"You like him. That CEO. It's not worth arguing with me over it," Susie continued as Fia tried to interrupt her, "I can tell. You were told someone at work was the father, and you could only think of him. He's the only person you see in that place, isn't he?"

"I-"

"Try a little experiment with me. Consider the alternatives. Isn't there another boss?"

"Darby," said Fia reluctantly. "But he's the nice one. He got me the job; he really had to persuade his cousin to let me work there."

"Is it nice for him to get you a job, when you're eventually framed for something while you are doing it?"

Fia stopped sharpening the pencils. "What?"

"And isn't he also related to your Mr Bard?"

"He's not my Mr Bard," she couldn't help the reply.

Susie chuckled. "What's this Darby like, then?"

"He's kind, friendly," Fia replied slowly. "He loves his family – his wife and daughters."

"Then he'd do anything to hide another child from them, right?"

Fia couldn't reply. Her brain had just opened

up a wide window of possibility that was impossible for her to process. She stabbed the pencil she was holding into a sheet of cardboard in front of her, so hard that the tip of it snapped on the table beneath.

"If you're right," she said, "If I've been set up by Darby from the beginning-"

"Calm down," said Susie. "Wait until you find out before you get angry. You could be wrong again. Ask Louella to help you find out, and then stand up for yourself, Fi."

"She can definitely help me," said Fia hotly, as her anger at the injustice continued to grow. "If Darby's to blame then it's her fault. She suggested the job there."

Susie laughed out loud. "Louella's never wrong though, right?"

"If she is this time, I'll never let her forget it."

CHAPTER TWENTY-ONE

The rain had finally stopped. It was coming to the end of the rainy season, and the temperature would soon drop. Fia held one end of the lead gently, and the fluffy puppy on the other end of it trotted delicately between the puddles on the pavement. It acted as though it hated to get its feet wet, and its fur remained spotless and finely-combed. Fia knew that if she'd gone to the countryside it would be covered in mud by now, and wondered how the animal managed to have two sides to its personality. She watched it carefully, waiting for it to turn on her, but it remained calm and poised, as though it could do better than its present company.

It was good to have a distraction. This was the first time she'd been back to the business district since she was fired several weeks ago, and the rhythm of her heart increased as she entered the shadows of the high-rises. It became harder to place one foot in front of another; her body just wanted to turn around and run.

I'm just walking the dog, she whispered to herself. I have every right to be here; they don't own the pavement.

The glass doors of JD Bard Associates shone in the weak sunshine, and Fia found the courage to walk up to them from somewhere. When they opened automatically she didn't enter, but just hovered in the space between them.

"I can't let you in," said Tony. He stood arms crossed in front of her, a towering figure of disapproval.

Fia took a tiny step backwards in apology. "I know. I'm sorry. I'm not here to visit the company - I was nearby walking the dog," she said. "I mean, I saw you and wondered how you were doing. I wanted to say hello."

Yes, she was here to say hello to Tony, the security guard. Susie was right, she should find out more about Darby Bard, and this was the man who saw all the comings and goings at the company; the man who waved down their taxis and saw the people who nestled in the back seats. He would know all the shadowy people, waiting for their lawyer. If anyone knew something that could help her, it would be Tony.

The puppy must have known it was being used as an excuse, because it took this moment to squat down outside the building and pee, creating a nice yellow puddle to match the ones made from rainwater. Tony raised his eyebrows, but said nothing about it.

"Not here," he said. "I'm on lunch break in twenty minutes. I'll meet you at the bagel shop on the corner."

"Okay," said Fia.

Tony suddenly straightened his shoulders, and Fia felt a coldness in the pit of her stomach. Joel Bard stood in the centre of the atrium, polished shoes on the polished floor, a watercolour outline behind the glass of the doors.

She knew there was a slight risk of meeting him here, but she'd told herself it was too unlikely. Joel Bard would work all hours of the day and night, and so he only spent a few minutes a day at reception. She cursed the unlucky timing. The awkwardness of it made her shrink inside her baggy hoodie, and curl her toes inside her worn tennis shoes.

Tony stepped back to activate the sensors, and the doors opened again. "I'm just moving her on, Mr Bard," he said.

His employer said nothing and simply stared

through the doors, his eyes locking with Fia's own. She immediately ached with the familiarity of it; the stern focus on his face that she had seen so many times before, the concentrated attention he gave her – but she soon realised how different it was now. There used to be heat in his gaze when he looked at her; Fia would feel her skin almost burning from it, but this time his eyes froze her to her bones. She'd never seen him so cold. And he stood so still, the only movement coming from the rapid rise and fall of his chest as he breathed.

Fia simply stared at him in reply and poured all her frustrated emotion into it, matching all the contempt he'd thrown at her over all the previous months and delivering it back to him the only way she could. She glared at him for what seemed half a life time, until he turned from her and walked away, becoming lost in the architecture of the entrance hall. Fia knew that he wouldn't leave the building until she was gone.

"Come on, fluff-ball," she said to the puppy, fighting down a sudden nausea. "Let's go and get a bagel." She tugged gently on the lead, hoping that Tony would make good on his promise and join her.

Tony did catch up with her sometime later, and by then Fia had managed to pull herself back together. It was embarrassing enough to think of all the nights she'd curled up in bed and sobbed over the past few weeks; no one was going to see her cry over Joel Bard.

They found a small wrought-iron table outside by the door of a little delicatessen, and sat down at it. Tony ordered an exceptionally sweet coffee with vanilla creamer and a delicate swirl of chocolate flakes on its surface. The cup almost completely disappeared into his muscled grip as he gently sipped at it.

"What?" he asked an amused Fia. "It's my favourite."

Fia tore off a small corner of her bagel and dropped it to the ground to keep the puppy entertained. It picked it up delicately and walked around in little circles, before settling down underneath her chair and munching as butter covered its nose. It looked completely harmless, but after their last outing, Fia knew better.

"Cute dog," said Tony. "What name does it go by?"

Fia hesitated. Although she's been spending quite some time with it since becoming unemployed, she still didn't remember its name. She tended to just call it Dog. Tony rolled his eyes, and flipped over the shiny disk on its collar.

"Fifi," he said. "Hello little Fifi. A guard dog you are not, but still adorable." He wiped her nose clean from butter, and Fifi looked at him with her liquid eyes.

"She's Louella's."

Tony nodded. "I've seen pictures. She's a proud parent. It's good to see you Fia, but I don't have long. Don't be polite - just tell me what you need."

This was Tony. Straight and to the point. Fia remembered that he didn't do small talk. But now he was here she didn't know where to start.

"I didn't do it," she said.

"I never said that you did," replied Tony calmly. "Not my place to make those decisions - not my job, not my strength. I leave the judgements to the other people in that building."

"Oh."

"We miss you at work," he said. "Got used to having you around. Any chance of it all being sorted yet?"

Fia shook her head. "I'm trying to fix it," she said. "I wanted to ask you something. It might be too confidential - you might not want to answer me."

Tony shrugged. "Then I won't. Try me." He put the small porcelain cup delicately back onto its saucer and gave her all his attention.

Fia bit the bullet. "Have you ever seen Darby Bard going into the offices with other women?" she asked.

Tony went very, very still. "Why do you want

to know?"

"He's a family man, right? Everyone says so. Honest and popular."

Tony bent down and tickled the puppy underneath its chin. It fawned on him at once, rolling over and showing its belly. The man began to give it a rough belly-rub, and a little pink tongue peeked out as the puppy yawned in happiness.

"He does like to be popular," he admitted quietly. "Lives on admiration, that one. It's a dangerous thing."

They sat in silence for a while as Fia finished her bagel. She wondered whether he was answering her question.

"Did I ever tell you about my wife?" he asked abruptly. "Wonderful woman. I never looked at another one the entire time I was with her. She passed ten years ago, and I still haven't looked. I can't stand cheaters. They're the worst."

"I'm sorry for your loss," said Fia.

He just shrugged again. "Darby Bard is a sucker for any woman that smiles at him. But as I said, it's not my place to judge another's life – we all have our own to lead. I won't say any more about it."

"What was your wife's name?"

"Francesca."

"It's a pretty name."

Tony smiled. "Don't worry too much. This

will all settle down. Everything passes eventually. When it has, don't be a stranger." He drained his cup. "I have to get back."

Fia gave him a little wave, and once she'd paid the bill she saw that the dog had fallen fast asleep, lulled by Tony's strokes and her full stomach. She sighed as she bent down to pick it up and carry it all the way back to the car park, its matchstick legs sticking out in all directions. She had to return her to her owner, and she was already late.

Louella had chosen a very strange meeting place to collect her little bundle of joy. Fia made her way through the snarled traffic until she reached the City Zoo, which stood right in the centre of the city, next to the green park that swam through the shopping district. Fia was a little late, and her friend was already waiting for her on a park bench which stood in a viewing station by a big wire fence.

There were two tigers inside the enclosure. One, the most docile, lay sunning itself under the cloudy sky. The other paced the bars, protecting its mate and completely ignoring the spectators who sat at the glass window and watched it. Its loose fur moved over its muscles, and made the stripes shiver in the afternoon air, and its giant paws seemed so soft, hiding the claws inside them.

"Why are we at the zoo?" asked Fia, sitting

down next to her.

"It was central. I had no idea where you were taking my little cutie today, and that's a first for me. I wouldn't let anyone else just head off with her – you are privileged, woman."

"But the park is right next door," objected Fia. "Wouldn't that be easier?"

"This is more... educational. I want to inspire Fifi to discover her inner wolf," replied Louella. "A woman can't spend her life being cute. She has to stand up for herself."

"That dog knows how to stand up for itself," said Fia with feeling. "I wouldn't worry so much about that."

"Nonsense, she's as pliable as anything; no backbone at all. I've never known her put a tiny paw out of place, have I, you adorable little baby girl?"

Louella held her arms out to her puppy. Its tail wagged in a happy little spiral as it tried to climb up her legs, and Fia was more than happy to hand the little dog back to her as she wondered what on earth had come over her severe friend.

"If you want her to be a stronger canine, then why are we looking at the cats?" she asked.

"Oh, this is for you." Louella shifted Fifi in her lap, and held her up to the tiger enclosure. "Look at the tigers, little sweetie-pie. Beautiful but dangerous. Auntie Fia needs to learn something from them."

The sleeping tiger raised its head and breathed in the air, ears twitching before it lay back down. The other one paused, one paw raised, before it continued its sweeping path around the enclosure. Fifi shivered.

"Is it a good idea, to wave her at them like that?" asked Fia. "I expect she's making them hungry. She's barely a mouthful to a tiger."

Louella snuggled the dog back down onto her lap, and sighed. "It's about time you fought back, Fia. I'm losing patience with you. I saw you speak to Tony, so I'm guessing you have a plan."

"Not really."

"Liar. Anyway, it doesn't matter. I'm throwing my hat into the ring. Whatever you want, I can do. I'm here to tell you that I'll stay your friend, whatever the situation."

Fia hesitated, then asked; "Can you get me into the office building tomorrow?"

Louella grinned. "Of course I can, chicken. That is literally my job. But we'll have to be careful; I suggest waiting until after the main rush at nine o'clock – how about ten o'clock tomorrow morning? It's best to get it over and done with. But now..." She stood up, and looked carefully at the pole on the pathway that had the collection of little signposts with animals on it, "It's time to educate little Fifi, and big

Fifi - let's go and visit the wolves. Pack mentality, yes? We are a team, and stronger together than we are apart."

"Susie called you about this, didn't she?"

"Yes, she absolutely did."

"I'll meet you at reception at ten tomorrow, then. I want to talk to Darby, and find out if he was the one who framed me."

Louella shrugged. "Then we'll track him down together. Come on."

"I don't think that the wolves are as exciting as the tigers," said Fia in a teasing tone as Louella began to walk away from her.

"Oh, I fancy their chances. I believe a pack of wolves can bring down a tiger if they work together, no matter how pretty its stripes are. Now, come and tell me what you want to do. I haven't got all day."

Fia stood up and followed her, and they wound their way through the thinning crowd of visitors. It wasn't long until the placed closed, and the younger families were already on their way home to feed the kids and put them to bed. The lull in the noise gave her time to think of something as they approached the wolves.

"Louella?"

"Yes?"

"Did you name that fluff-ball after me?"

"It's a tradition in Charly's family to name a

baby after its godmother," said Louella with a smile. "Welcome to the family."

The tiny creature in Louella's arms looked up at Fia with a smug expression behind its black, beady eyes, while she wondered what on earth she'd done in a previous life to deserve such an honour. It continued to stare at her over Louella's shoulders all the way to their destination, but she refused to break eye contact with it first. It was only when Louella reached the wolf enclosure that the dog eventually looked away, and as Fia looked up she suddenly recognised one of the people inside the viewing station. She cursed.

"What is it?" Louella asked.

Fia pointed at the crowd. "James," she said. "He's the only person I gave my signature to, after I started at the company. He must have collected it for Darby, so he could forge it on all those documents. He knows about everything his boss gets up to, after all."

Louella whistled, and Fifi's ears pricked up. "He must have known about it, of course he must... and so, he was an accessory to the crime. Well, I've got to be honest; I didn't think that streak of bacon had it in him. What a dirtbag. And now, of course, I'm very embarrassed that I introduced him to you in the first place - do you need me to make up for being such a bad friend? Just say the word."

Fia waved her anger away. "Of course not. I'm just really surprised to see him here."

"As am I - he should be with the weasels, don't you think? He's punching way above his weight in this company. Who's the girl with him?"

"His new girlfriend. He met her at a bookshop."

"Of course he did." Louella squinted at the pair in front of them, "Well, she needs to know what sort of man she's dealing with. Do you want to let her down gently, or shall I?"

Fia sighed. "It's my mess, I'll deal with it - lend me your engagement ring, won't you?"

Louella twisted it from her finger, the giant diamond glinting in the low sunlight as she handed it over. "Lose it, and you'll die," she said, matter-of-factly.

"I won't," Fia promised, and approached the couple, who were holding hands and gazing at the pack of wolves that lay huddled together in the middle of their enclosure. The smell of wolf musk wafted through the wire of the fence on the late afternoon breeze, and Fia immediately began a list in her head of all the places that were more romantic than this. It was endless.

CHAPTER TWENTY-TWO

James jumped the minute that Fia walked in front of him, and she'd never been more certain of someone's guilt, but she ignored the expression on his face and zeroed in on the clasped hands between the couple.

"What's this?" she demanded, her eyes filling with tears. "Are you out enjoying yourself, James? Without a single thought of what I'm going through?"

Her target froze, but he was intelligent enough not to say anything. He wasn't going to incriminate himself, thought Fia, not until he knew what she'd discovered. This was a man who used people. She looked up, into the eyes of the kind woman who stood beside him.

"Who are you?" she demanded. "And what

are you doing with my future husband?" She held up her left hand and fanned out her fingers, the diamond visible from a mile away. For such a serious woman, Louella really did go overboard when she loved someone.

"I-" the woman dropped James' hand as though it was on fire, but she held her ground, her face uncertain. "Who are you?" she asked.

Fia ignored her. "What were you thinking, during all those long hours at the law firm?" she demanded. "All that overtime; were you really working, or were you lying to me? Did you think I wouldn't notice - that I was too dumb to figure it out? Did you think you were going to get away with it? What about poor little me, sitting at home and waiting for a phone call?"

James didn't even slightly wilt beneath her barrage of questions. "You don't know half of the things I've done," he replied softly, "In the name of my career. And you should be grateful that you were at home; a busy work environment is no place for a woman, after all. You should have let the men handle it from the beginning."

"If we weren't in public," Fia hissed, "I'd slap you in both your faces."

The girlfriend had taken several steps away, distancing herself from the spectacle that Fia and James were creating. The few people left in the crowd weren't even pretending to look at the wolves now; the only person that was interested in them was Louella, who was holding Fifi up to the enclosure and whispering in her ear, supremely unbothered by Fia's actions behind her.

"He's no good," Fia advised the woman. "He's a cheater. You don't need to believe me, of course – stay with him if you want to. But if I were you, I'd leave him here and never speak to him again."

The woman was pulling James away, and asking questions. He was answering, but she barely let him finish each stuttering sentence. Then she was turning on her heel, and walking away from James, who just stood there and waited for her to come back. When it was obvious that she wasn't going to turn around he took off down the path after her, calling her name frantically and waving his arms. They soon disappeared behind a ring of hedges, and Fia breathed a sigh of relief.

There was a gentle tugging on her ring finger, and Fia helped Louella slide the engagement ring off so she could put it firmly back in place on her own hand. Her friend then stood next to her with her arms crossed, Fifi sniffing around her ankles, and huffed.

"Look at him. The man can't even run - it's pathetic. Now, let's go back to the car; I shall allow you to drive me home. We can discuss the details

223

about tomorrow on the way."

"Fine," said Fia, overwhelmed with the support her friend was giving her in her time of need. On a normal day, Louella wouldn't be seen dead in her ancient Micra – and this reminded her of something. "I can't believe you threatened me with death," she muttered, as they headed for the car park.

"If you lost the ring? Oh, I wouldn't have done it." Her friend reassured her. "Charly would. She's a demon, that woman, I assure you."

Louella barely rummaged behind the reception desk the following morning before she found a spare pass for the offices. It was almost as if she'd prepared one just for this very occasion. Fia placed the lanyard around her neck, and straightened it to match her neat clothes. She was back in her office finery - silk blouse and pencil skirt, hair swept up and high heels on. The fine stitching was still uncomfortable, but she could see why women wore it as armour - as she'd dressed this morning, she'd felt her work persona settling around her once more. She was ready to fight.

Tony was the only other person in the atrium as she headed to the check-in gates, but he seemed to be struck with a bad case of temporary blindness. Fia knew he wouldn't actively help her, but he was obviously taking his motto of 'live and let live' seriously. He became very interested in a stain on the floor as she walked by, and didn't even glance in her direction. Fia wondered what Louella had bribed him with.

Darby would be in the penthouse office. Fia hadn't been given any reason to visit it while she was working here, and she had no idea what awaited her on the top floor. It was obvious to her now, just how off-limits Darby kept his private self; how important he thought he was. She thought of Joel Bard then, working through the night to help people on the seventh floor, close at hand in times of trouble. It was a complete contrast, and she wondered how she could have got them both so wrong.

A cheerful persona, she thought to herself, doesn't make a man a saint. And a grump can still change the world.

"Do you have your phone?" Louella asked. Fia nodded, tapping the pocket of her skirt. "Good," she said. "Call me if you need anything at all."

The pass had worked well, granting her access to the executive floor, and Fia unlocked her phone as she approached the door of the penthouse. She pressed the record key, and slipped it back into her pocket. Then she knocked on the door.

"Enter," said Darby, his friendly voice calling out from the other side.

The penthouse office was cluttered, and

colourful. It couldn't be more different from Joel Bard's office if it tried. Bright red shelving units broke the huge space up into different areas, and they were stuffed to the edges with stacks of dog-eared paperwork. Statues and knick-knacks scattered themselves over dressers and tables. The small amount of wall space that remained free from furniture was covered in shiny posters of different mountains, their snow-capped peaks giving the room a feeling of height without anyone needing to even glance out of the window.

"I've climbed them all, of course," said Darby, with a wry smile. "It's important to stay fit, and keep a hobby. I've been to the highest point on every continent, and stared down at the land beneath me – it's a wonderful feeling. I guess you haven't had a chance to travel the world much, have you? I saw some rare eagles on my last trip; I wish I'd been able to take an egg back with me."

"I saw tigers yesterday at the zoo," replied Fia sarcastically, picking up a statue from the table to examine it more closely. She didn't feel any impulse to be polite; it really didn't bother her if anyone thought badly of her here anymore. The statue was a little polo player on a pony. It was incredibly tacky.

Darby watched her closely. "Ah, all these little souvenirs I seem to collect. I don't dare let the cleaners in anymore; this amount of dusting is far above their pay grade."

Or you're hiding things from them, thought Fia. "Do you play polo, when you're not climbing mountains?" she asked.

"No; they're all gifts from grateful clients. It's embarrassing really, but they do like to express their appreciation and I can't bring myself to throw any of them away -what can I do?"

Fia placed the statue carefully back down in the exact spot she'd picked it up from. Darby was sitting on a little sofa that was pulled out into a futon. He was nestled into the cushions with a glass in one hand and a tablet in the other. The contents of the glass looked suspiciously like red wine. It wasn't yet eleven o'clock in the morning.

"Do you know, I'm just going over my diary and I can't see you in it," he remarked, tapping the screen with his wine glass before he swallowed another mouthful. "How on earth did you get in here? I shall have to interview the staff."

"You didn't take my pass away when I left," Fia lied quickly.

Darby hummed. "Let's just say I didn't. Have you brought me my money back?"

"You know I don't have it."

A frustrated sigh, and he dropped the tablet onto the cushions beside him. "Look, if you've come here to protest your innocence again, then you're wasting your time. I've been nice enough - I restrained my inequitable cousin, and bought you some temporary freedom. You should be grateful, right?"

He looked up at her then, and the friendly mask he wore fell from his face a bit. He rubbed at his curly hair in irritation. It really did look so similar to Michael's.

"He looks like you, doesn't he?"

"My cousin?"

"No. Your son, Michael. You have the same hair."

Silence from the sofa. Fia didn't see the need to rush him; she wasn't going anywhere until he'd talked. She contented herself with pottering around the shelves, watching him wince as she made a move for the paperwork. Ah. He was hiding a lot of information in here, then.

"Take your time," she said. "I haven't got anywhere else to be. I'm very recently unemployed."

"Fine," the answer came at last. "You're a smart one, aren't you? I knew it was a wise decision to hire you. But you don't have the full story, Fia. You don't know how much it would hurt that boy if my family knew he existed. You must understand, I did everything in his best interest."

Devastation was writ across Darby's face. He looked so sincere that Fia hesitated. She thought of

Michael, and the ridiculous wealth of the Bard family; it was possible that Darby knew more about keeping him safe than she did. She wondered whether his parents were strict and old-fashioned, whether they'd want to hide the boy away more than anyone else would, whether they would be ashamed of his existence.

Darby took this moment of silence to rise wanly from the sofa. "And look at me; I'm so worried about that poor little boy that I'm drinking in the morning. It's awful, isn't it, what a man can be reduced to? Now, I'm going outside, to get some fresh air - so I'm afraid that if you want to keep this conversation going, you'll have to come with me."

He pulled back the heavy curtain that covered a floor-length window that ran down one side of the penthouse, and stepped through it onto a wide balcony. Fia felt she had no choice but to follow him; she didn't have nearly enough recorded for a confession; his admitting to being Michael's father wouldn't get her off the hook for the fraud investigation. She lifted the corner of her phone from her pocket, just enough to check that it was still recording, and once she was sure that she hadn't knocked it and turned it off she followed him through the window.

The height hit her all at once; they were almost as high up as she'd been on the dance floor on the night of the award ceremony, but she'd felt safer up there than she did now, on this small space that projected from the side of the building. She was too high up to even smell the pollution of the City, everything was ozone and cold air.

Darby was draped over the rails on the far side, a complete picture of dejection, but when Fia looked at him closely she didn't believe in the act at all. "Did you pay off his mother with the money you stole from the company?" she asked. "I know you didn't use it to find Michael a safe place to live. You just abandoned him."

"No one will believe you, you know," remarked Darby sadly, watching the birds nesting in the balcony opposite. "Least of all my cousin. If your ambition led in that direction I'd think again. We're a team, and we always have been. He'll side with me."

"I'll find the evidence."

"I hardly think so. I was so clever at hiding it, you see."

Fia started at this - she'd almost given up hoping that he would admit to it out loud; she'd begun to think he was just too clever to be pinned down. He pushed away from the railings and moved behind her, pulling the windows closed in one swift movement. Fia heard a click as they locked. Then he approached her as he continued, before whispering intimately into her ear.

"I had you earmarked for the fall before you even began to work here. What other reason would I possibly have for hiring you? You're woefully unqualified for the job - my cousin was right about that. He's far better at sticking to the rules than I am. You should have listened to him more."

"I..." but what could she say? He was right; she was terrible at surviving here; she hadn't seen this coming at all.

"If you had any sense at all, you'd forget about it – you had no intention of staying here long-term anyway, so I've hardly damaged your career prospects. And you managed to charm Joel just enough for him to let you off the hook, which was smart; and it's made my plan even easier. Maybe I *do* owe you something."

"You let people think I was a thief!"

"True. And a good thief would get something for their trouble, I suppose. How about a little bit of money for you too, and then you keep your mouth shut? Otherwise, I might begin to get a little angry."

Darby took hold of her and pulled her towards him, using so much force that Fia felt as though she sank an inch into the ground. He was a lot stronger than she'd thought, and almost as tall as his cousin; maybe it hadn't been sensible to be alone with him like this. A quick glance to the exterior walls confirmed that there were no security cameras on this

231

balcony, which must be why Darby wanted to move their conversation away from his office.

"There's nothing you have that I want," she gasped. "You can't pay me off." Fia clutched at her phone through the fabric of her pocket, ready to sacrifice the recording to call someone for help, but then she heard someone banging on the glass.

"Hey!" A shout came from the other side of the window.

Fia stood on tip-toe and peered over her captor's shoulder. It was Joel Bard. She was standing far too close to his cousin; there was barely an inch between them. He would think that they were together, she was sure of it. This looked very bad.

"Let go of her, Darby."

Darby laughed and cupped her face, moving it towards his own. "You're interrupting us, Joel. Fia just came to me unexpectedly this morning. She was just explaining what she would do to clear her name. Did you know that she was that sort of woman?"

Fia twisted her face and pulled at his fingers, but his hold on her was absolute. She could feel the pressure of it bruising her as he tightened his grip on the lower half of her face.

"I said, let go." Joel Bard managed to open the clasp on the French windows at last, and he swung them open.

"Why don't you make me?" Darby asked

him, sweetly. He swung Fia around until she felt the small of her back hit the low rail that ran around the balcony. Now those thin bars of metal were the only thing preventing her from falling for over thirty floors, and landing messily onto the tarmac below. "Oh, right. You won't come out here. We're a bit too high up for you, aren't we?"

"Darby, I'm warning you-"

"Oh, don't worry about what happens to her, will you? I'll explain it later, Joel. Why is this bothering you so much? She's stolen from us, and you were never that keen on her."

Fia tried to speak, but she couldn't open her jaw. Darby chuckled when he felt her try, and quietly shushed her. She stamped hard on his foot, and he finally let go of her as he cried out in pain.

"He did it!" she cried. "He stole the money; I haven't touched anything."

"Liar."

He slapped her in retaliation, and as Fia reeled backwards from the sharp sting of it she leaned a bit too far over the edge. A light of inspiration showed in Darby's eyes for a brief second as she locked her gaze with his. No. He wouldn't push her; he wouldn't go that far even in this desperate situation.

But he wasn't pulling her back, either. Fia struggled to stand upright in her slippery high heels, promising herself to bin them all and live in sneakers for the rest of her life, if she was lucky enough to survive this. A slow grin crossed Darby's features like a snake crawling through grimy desert sand, and Fia began to fall.

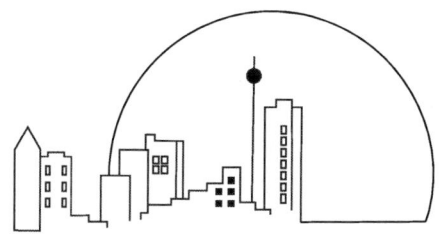

CHAPTER TWENTY-THREE

A hand gripping her wrist, and she was upright once more. A stable body to lean against; warm and solid. Joel Bard had crossed the balcony, and he stood between her and his cousin with a wry smile.

"Back off, Darby. Don't make me hit you; we are related, after all."

Fia recognised the performance, now she looked for it. Joel Bard looked as put-together as he had onstage at the awards night; a mask of relaxed professionalism – but she could see the blood draining from his face, the wooden way he looked at Darby as he carefully avoided the view beyond the rooftop.

"What are you doing?" Darby asked in shock.

"Did you really think I wouldn't question this?

That I wouldn't look into it, and find out the paper trail was false? Did you really think I could just blindly believe you, when that amount of money was missing, and you blamed her for it?"

You've always believed me before..."

"You're breaking the law, cousin. I'm ashamed to be working with you."

Darby's face twisted, and for a moment there was no trace of friendliness in him at all. "How long have you been listening?" he asked.

"Long enough."

"I'm not going to let that little boy ruin everything we've worked for," he said. "I don't think you want that, either. You know the family won't accept that bastard."

"I should think he'll be accepted with open arms," Joel Bard remarked. "It's you that will be in trouble. I'd forgotten how hard you worked to cover your tracks when we were in school together. That's my fault. We should never have worked together."

"You're very lucky to be working with me," Darby spat. "And I don't think you'll say anything once you've thought it through. Do you think it's easy, managing everyone's expectations? Keeping everybody happy? I'm the glue that holds this place together – the oil that makes it run. I may not manage as many cases as you do, but this company couldn't exist without me. When was the last time you spoke to another company owner without pissing them off?"

Joel Bard grabbed Darby's shirt, and it bunched at the seams as Darby was briefly lifted off his feet. "You're poisoning this company," he said. "Don't piss me off any more than you have done; I don't want to be explaining your bruises to my aunt. She'll be cross enough when she finds out you kept her away from her grandson."

"You wouldn't-"

He dropped him. Darby's legs folded beneath him as he sat on the concrete of the roof and Fia watched him deflate.

"It's time to grow up and be a man, Darby. I'll give you a week. Find the money by then, and replace it all. I'll offer you the same deal you gave Fia; it seems only fair. But if I'm unlucky enough to see your face again, I'm re-arranging it."

"You aren't thinking clearly," Darby said with confidence. "It's your fear of heights, colouring your thinking. When you're back on the ground you'll realise I'm right."

"It's been a long time since I got lost on the side of that mountain as a boy, Cousin, and this is a building, not a rock-face. I'm doing just fine now. You're out of excuses."

"I wish they'd never found you," Darby muttered. "I wish I'd pushed you further down, when I left you there. You've been in my way ever since, just like I knew you would be."

Joel Bard said nothing else to him, his mouth set closed and his hands gripped into fists. "Can you walk?" he asked Fia, and she realised these were the first words he'd said to her in a month.

She unsnapped the buckles on her heels and slid them from her feet, abandoning them on the rooftop. "Yes," she replied.

They left Darby there alone. Joel Bard put one careful hand to her waist, guiding her through the opening doors of the elevator. She wedged herself into the corner as it descended through all the floors of the building, just to make sure that he wouldn't touch her again. He leaned against the metal of it, his face white and drawn, silent from the realisation that Darby had abandoned him on a mountainside as a child.

Even though she was angry at him for firing her, Fia couldn't bear to see him like that. She cast around her for anything to say that would snap him out of it.

"It takes forever to ride this elevator the entire way. What a waste of floors. Do you own this building too?" she finally asked.

"Yes."

"So you really are a *rich* asshole," she said.

Joel Bard's lips twitched at the welcome insult, but he didn't say anything. He looked her up and down as though memorising her instead, until his vision came to rest on her bare feet. Fia curled up her toes and pretended to ignore him until the doors opened on the ground floor.

The sound of heels tapping around the corner. Louella appeared, out of breath and her clothes askew.

"Mr Bard, did you-"

"I found her," he answered shortly. "I got there in time."

"You called him?" Fia shot her a look that was so loaded with venom that she was surprised Louella didn't shrivel up into a dried husk of shame.

"Yes," she admitted. "I did it when we got here. I thought if you got a confession from Darby, he should hear it."

"I heard it." Joel Bard nodded firmly in confirmation, a dark cloud over his face. "I just hope he doesn't cause us further trouble. I'll get all the evidence together as quickly as I can, don't worry."

"I recorded everything he said," Fia held up her mobile phone. "I'll send Louella a copy, you can ask her for it."

Joel Bard was still very quiet. "If you take my number, could you send it to me directly?" he asked, a small humble note threading through the question.

She supposed this made sense. "But I want my name cleared," she said.

"Of course. And your job back, I'm guessing?"

Fia almost felt a twinge of sympathy for him, then. He'd lost the support of his cousin, and she could understand why he needed people he could trust around him. She looked around at the shiny surfaces, the impersonal beauty of the décor. She almost wanted to come back; to help him again, but he hadn't been there for her when she needed it. Neither of them had trusted the other when it mattered – they didn't have that kind of relationship.

"No," she said, "I never want to step inside this building again."

She threw professionalism to the wind, and gave Louella a sudden hug and a whispered goodbye. Louella simply patted her on the back, and told her to get home safe.

She was very distracted by the warm pavement burning beneath her bare feet as she hunted for a taxi, and so it wasn't until she got home that Fia realised that neither of them had taken the all-access pass back from her before she left; it still hung around her neck. That couldn't be accidental, but it was a silent invitation that she never intended to use.

The small bars by the riverside re-opened as the flooding from the rains went down, and their owners soon unrolled their brightly-striped awnings again, and opened for business. Once Susie saw the postage-stamp fabric stretch from building to building, she rang Fia and suggested a night out to celebrate her victory. She invited Louella along as well, and so they sat on the chairs scattered over the damp flagstones together the following evening, sharing a bottle of cheap fizz out between three plastic glasses, toasting each other as though it was champagne.

"Congratulations," said Louella, heroically trying to get a clinking sound from the plastic as she tapped her glass against Fia's. "Here's to a bastard man getting what he deserves, and to your re-ignited writing career. Now, that's quite difficult to pronounce after a few glasses of this stuff, isn't it? Still, we're both happy for you," Susie nodded along with Louella's words, "But it's lonely without you at the company. I shall make do, of course, but I'm not entirely happy about it."

"I expect lots of the other people are happy though," replied Fia. "I made some amazing mistakes."

"True, but I'm used to those. After all the time I've known you, this is just one occasion in a long line of-"

Susie tapped her on the nose when she said this; her early fear of Louella completely gone. Fia took the opportunity to steal her drink.

"Hey!" Louella reached for the bottle, and

refilled them all. "I was just going to say, don't be so sure, Fi. I think there's someone at that law firm that misses you more than you think."

"That wasn't really me," said Fia shortly. "This is me." She gestured to her dungarees, and her damp sneakers. The table fell quiet, and she changed the subject quickly. "Anyway, it doesn't matter. I wanted to meet you both for a reason - now I'm writing again, I wanted to ask Susie something."

"What do you need?" Susie rolled her sleeves up, and tried to look ready for business.

"An illustrator for my new book. Would you do it for me?"

"Me? Why me?"

"I can't think of anyone better."

Susie pretended to think about it, and then proposed another toast. "To future collaborations, and hours of sketches!" she called, and they all drank.

"Don't put your glasses down yet, girls," Louella advised, shaking the bottle experimentally, and squeezing the last few drops of it into their glasses. "Honestly, I think we'll need another bottle of this soon, we're getting through it rather quickly. Now, I have some news of my own, and a request for advice. Are you ready?"

They were, and so Louella told them that she and Charly were finally tying the knot.

"You know we've been engaged for quite a

while; we just haven't told our families yet. The reception is booked for next year," she said. Susie, Fia and Fifi were to be the bridesmaids.

"I'm too old," objected Fia. "I can't walk down the aisle next to my goddaughter."

Susie snorted through her champagne. "You'll have to deal with it. If it helps, I'll hold onto her lead, it you're too worried about the responsibility. What harm could the little thing do?"

"Don't ask," replied Fia with feeling, although she thought it would probably be alright if there wasn't a large body of water next to the church.

"There's no need," said Louella, coolly. "I'm training her to walk it herself. She'll look fabulous."

"What about the table decorations?" asked Susie with a frown.

"Well, I was hoping you'd be able to help us with that..."

Fia left them to the wedding discussion when their thoughts began to turn to bridesmaid dresses, and she climbed the concrete wall that separated the riverbank from the fast-flowing water, swelled from the months of rain. She sipped at the sharp, cold bubbles in her glass, and remembered the last time she'd left a party early, and another wall she'd sat on.

What would she do if he was here now? Sitting on the wall beside her, in a wet shirt with that inviting smile in his eyes? He'd tease her about her dungarees, and be comfortable to lean on. His shoulder muscles would be hard underneath his shirt. She could make him hard in other places, too.

He wouldn't join in with all the conversation, but he'd buy her friends an expensive bottle of champagne without batting an eye about it. He'd arrange for a company car to take them all home, so they didn't have to bother finding a taxi. He'd take her back to his immaculate apartment, and she wouldn't leave until the morning...

And that was the problem. The two of them were from completely different backgrounds. She'd judged him based on her own experiences, and he'd done the same to her; it was impossible to meet in the middle now. It was best to avoid him; it was over between them. Fia was just happy that the misunderstanding was over, and she wished him happy.

Snatches of conversation rose from the table beneath her. Talk of colours, and fabrics. Whether both of the brides would carry flowers, whether it was animal cruelty to make a small dog wear shoes. Fia smiled, and climbed down from the wall to join them, calling for another cheap bottle of house wine from the waiter walking past the tables. It would taste better than anything else possibly could with the company she was keeping. Joel Bard could keep his fine vintages. He could stay inside his glass tower, safely shut away from her.

There was only one problem with Fia's decision. Joel Bard had a mind of his own, and his morals were obviously slipping. Fia had sent the voice file over to him as soon as she'd got home, hoping to leave all of the memories of Darby behind her. But of course, that now meant that her ex-boss knew her mobile number. She thought he would leave their acquaintance like that, and if she'd known for one moment that he would actually dare to call her on it, she would have asked Louella to send the file in her place.

The first time her phone rang, it was early in the morning, and the sun had barely risen. Fia dragged it out from beneath her pillow when she was half-way between asleep and awake, thinking it was her alarm. She clicked the 'accept' button before she realised what she was doing.

"Hello?" she asked, trying to clear the sleep from her voice.

"Good morning," his voice came through the telephone. "Did you sleep well?"

Fia blinked rapidly, trying to focus as she double-checked the caller ID. It was still blurry, but she could just make out the three letters 'CEO'. She frowned.

"What?" she muttered.

"I must have offended you more than I thought," said Joel Bard thoughtfully, "If I'm a 'what', now, and not a 'who'."

"I *meant* what time is it."

"Oh."

Fia yawned, and rolled over in the bed.

"It's five o'clock," he said quietly into her ear. "I'm sorry for waking you."

"What made you call me this early? Did you think about me the moment you woke up?"

"Something like that."

"I was being sarcastic."

"I wasn't."

He fell silent then, and she could hear his gentle breathing down the phone, relaxed and steady. As she held the phone to her ear, it sounded as though it came from the pillow beside her, and it was too close, and too intimate.

"Do you need something?" she asked, the pause beginning to nettle her.

"You."

"Why? Are you angry, or upset?"

He sighed. "Neither. I'm just thinking about you. I want to know that you're okay."

Well, that was easily solved. "I am," she said.

"Good-"

"I'm going back to sleep," she told him. "Goodnight."

Fia fumbled to hang up the call, watching the screen of her phone go dark as she buried her head in the blankets to hide from the dawn that was trying to peep through the blinds of her apartment. She checked the call history, just to make sure that her imagination wasn't playing tricks with her, just to double-check that she wasn't dreaming. Then she lay still, and closed her eyes, counting back slowly from ten.

It didn't work, and sleep continued to evade her. Eventually, she gave it up as a lost cause, and contented herself with an early morning jog instead. If her feet hit the pavement a little harder than usual, well. No one would know.

It had seemed so natural, when she was barely awake, for his voice to be the one that woke her up. It was eye-opening to think that his company was only one button-click away, and that he thought that he missed her. Fia reminded herself that he didn't, that they were completely different people, and that he didn't know her at all.

She ran until she reached the river and followed the pathway next to it, along the centre of the canyon that the City sprawled through, out towards the ocean. She ran until her energy was almost gone, until her legs ached, and she could barely walk back home, but she could still hear his voice in her ears. This could get addictive. Fia didn't answer his calls again.

Soon, missed call notifications would drop into her phone like confetti. They would occasionally appear at lunchtimes, but would most often show in the early mornings, blinking there for her to acknowledge as soon as she woke up. Within a week, Fia was intimately aware of Joel Bard's waking schedule, which frustrated the hell out of her.

There were no evening calls. He was obviously too busy wining and dining all the clients, now Darby wasn't there to do it. She hoped he was having fun with all those glamorous people; maybe he would meet someone special there, someone cool and collected, like he was. They could be a City power couple, making deals and whispering in people's ears at social events. Good luck to them both.

Until that happened, she would ignore her phone every time his caller ID appeared; she'd let it ring, and wait for the answerphone to kick in. He never left a voice message, just another little notification on her phone. She certainly didn't count them. It took him a long time to get the hint, but within a fortnight the phone calls stopped altogether, and Fia breathed freely again.

Until the little text messages started arriving. The missed calls turned into 'good morning', and 'remember an umbrella, it's raining today'. There were no questions for her to answer, he wasn't that shameless, there was nothing for her to respond to. Of course, she thought about blocking him, and her thumb hovered over the icon to do it more than once.

I can't upset Louella's boss, she told herself. I owe it to my friend to be nice, what if I have to go and see her at work one day, if there's an emergency?

It was an easy excuse. She found herself smiling at more than one of them, but reminded herself not to get used to it. They'd end soon enough, just as the phone calls had.

CHAPTER TWENTY-FOUR

They did stop, in the end. Fia told herself she was glad about it. She enjoyed three days of blissful silence, until there was a knock on her front door one late evening. It made her jump as it broke her chain of thought. She was at her writing desk, deep in a scene of her latest book, with only one day left before she had to send it to her editor.

The fairies and imps inside her imagination popped like bubbles. The mountainside that they sat in swirled away from her as those few knocks on the door interrupted her scene, and brought her back to reality. Fia hoped it wasn't Susie. She knew better than to come here without calling first, and she wasn't due for another hour; she had to finish this before they could discuss illustrating it together. The knocks sounded again.

Perhaps it was her landlord. Fia cracked the front door, opening until the safety chain pulled tight, letting in the coolness of the late evening air.

"Who is it?"

Expensive leather shoes. Jeans, and a heavy-weave T-shirt. Joel Bard's face above the ensemble. He knew where she lived.

"Of course I do," his expression said. "You filled in an application form to work for me, didn't you?"

Fia didn't remove the chain.

"Can I come in?" he asked in the end.

She sighed, and opened the door; she had no defence to counteract such politeness. And he must have planned ahead to see her, she knew casual clothes didn't come easily to him.

"Did you come to see me?" she asked, cursing the obviousness of her question. She covered her confusion by waving the kettle at him. When he nodded in acceptance, she rummaged in the cupboard for the teapot that she kept for company.

Joel Bard seemed content to roam her tiny apartment. It couldn't compare to his own; it was on the rougher side of town, two floors up a rickety fire escape and the size of a matchbox. Fia winced when he stuck his head into her bathroom, and wished she'd hidden her old clothes and her razor.

He'd stopped wandering when she came out of her postage-stamp kitchen, and was flicking through some sketchbooks that sat beside her laptop.

"For a man that likes his privacy, you aren't shy about poking into other people's." Fia handed him a cup of tea, and he blew on it.

"These sketches-"

"Yes?" Fia sat down, but he didn't follow her lead. He hovered in the centre of the space, still unsure of his welcome.

"They're by Paul Devlin."

"They are."

He flicked through page after page, absorbed in the line work. He seemed to have forgotten the reason for his visit completely. "But he painted landscapes. Skylines... Why do you have a book full of dragons?"

"He painted them for me. For my writing."

Joel Bard compared her notebooks to Paul's illustrations. "This is impressive." He noticed the surnames then, and the photograph by her sofa. "He was your brother?" He barely waited for Fia's confirmation before repeating himself; "He drew dragons? How strange."

"It's not that strange to have an imagination. Not everyone needs to be serious all the time."

He snapped the book shut at that. "I need to apologise to you."

"No need." Fia just wanted him to stop talking. "I thought worse things about you. I thought that you would actually abandon a child, did you know that? I thought you were Michael's father, not Darby. We just didn't know each other at all, and I'm the one who's sorry."

"Sorry we spent time together? Or with the way it ended?"

"It had to end. We both knew what we were getting in to, didn't we?" she asked.

"I didn't." His hands shook, and the tea spilled.

An angry red mark blossomed on his wrist, but he didn't even wince. Fia shook the last drops of hot liquid from it at once, and wrapped his hand in a cold, wet cloth once she had soaked it in the sink. He placed his other hand on top of hers, holding her firmly in place.

"I want to be with you," he said.

"You don't trust me. I don't trust you."

"I do trust you now; it just took me a while. I always knew you weren't capable of such a thing..."

"You didn't when it counted. You had to think about it."

"I think about everything, and I always find the evidence first. You know that." He gently brushed the hair from her face, and pulled her closer with his burned hand, not caring at all about the pain. "I can make you trust me. Anything you want to know..."

She could feel his breath on her cheek, the warmth of the cinnamon cologne rising from the softness of his T-shirt. He should dress like this more often, it suited him.

"You ignored me for weeks," she said.

"And you've done the same to me."

"You don't want me," she whispered.

"You can refuse me, but you can't decide for me," his lips were moving against her cheek now. "I'm a very decisive man. I always know what I want."

Fia shivered, and involuntarily moved into him. An accidental kiss brushed against her as his mouth made slow contact with her cheek, just catching the corner of her mouth. He pressed another one against her, and she shuddered in response.

"You don't know anything about me," she objected, pushing him away.

"I know more than you think. And I can do my research. I'm good at that."

He tipped her chin up, his mouth aligning with hers. Fia didn't know what to do, it seemed like they were two magnets when they were together. She didn't want to fight it anymore, and their lips were almost touching.

Another knock at the front door. Fia jumped, and Joel Bard released his hold on her at once.

"Susie," she said. "She's her to talk about the

illustrations. You have to go."

Disappointment stained his face; it was impossible for him to hide his small expressions from her now she knew how to read them.

"But I think I-"

"Go back. Don't you have enough to do? You can't have time to waste on me."

Another knock at the door, and Fia couldn't be more grateful. She almost ran to it, throwing it open and engaging Susie in excited conversation the moment she stepped into the room. It was as though Joel Bard wasn't there at all.

He just stood there patiently, and listened to them talk. Susie was the first to finally acknowledge him again, and she did so with a wicked look in her eye, curiosity oozing from every pore.

"Mr Bard! How... interesting to see you here, visiting Fia. Am I in the way? Should I come back in a little while?"

Fia merely shrugged. She knew she was being petty, but really, she had no idea what to say. Joel Bard saved the moment, of course. He'd probably had lots of practice since he'd been left alone at the company.

"Ah, no please stay. My errand is done - I just came to say thank you. And I mean it," he caught Fia by the sleeve. "Thank you. It has been hard without Darby, I can't lie, but you helped me open my eyes to his behaviour. It's going to take a while to remove all his poison from the firm, but without you he would still be there. Thank you."

He'd actually thanked her for something. She felt her cheeks glow, and hoped Susie hadn't noticed as she pulled her arm free and muttered a 'welcome'. She didn't say anything else to him, and so after he struggled through a brief but polite conversation with Susie, he made his excuses and left, defeated.

"Well," said Susie. "He's sincere, isn't he? He looks at you like you're a slice of gateaux and he's lost his spoon. When did you start dating?"

"We're not dating. Come and look at the picture designs."

Fia slid the chain back onto the door with force, just in case he came back again. Susie made calming noises, and drank Fia's tea.

"Fine, fine. My lips are sealed. I'll just have this; the buses around here are so dusty, and I'm parched. You can drink the other one that you made; you looked close enough to the previous owner of it to cope with his germs. Drink up, it's still hot."

Fia drank the rest of Joel Bard's tea, and changed the subject.

Everything stopped, then. There were no more calls, no texts. It took Fia some time to stop looking for the messages first thing in the morning.

The year turned, and Susie gifted her a giant knitted scarf for Christmas. Fia could wrap it around herself twice, and she needed to; the wind cut through the loops of the wool like refrigerated needles.

Fia's agent arranged a small launch party for her latest book, at the little independent bookstore on the outskirts of town that she's been to with James earlier in the year. It was good to be back there, to be the one with the new release. Fia finally felt like herself again. There were glossy posters of all the characters standing throughout the store, and a large table covered in first editions ready for her to sign at the end of the event. She got there an hour before it started, too nervous to wait any longer.

Susie arrived even earlier than she did, a proud first-time illustrator, and the two of them wasted time re-arranging the piles of books on the table just to look busy. The bright front covers cheered the room up as much as the Christmas tree in the corner did. Her style was very different to Paul's, and her drawings of cheeky pixies with round faces filled the space, covering the bookshelves.

"Paul would have loved these," Fia told her. "They're great."

Tears welled up in Susie's eyes. "Thank you for saying so. But you know he'd never have said that out loud. He's have found every flaw in them that he could."

"But he wouldn't have meant it, that was just his style. I think this one is my favourite." Fia tapped the poster next to her. The curly-haired elf that sat on a ladybird looked suspiciously like Michael. "Did you get inspiration for these from your students?"

"A little bit. Cute, aren't they? I've invited a lot of them here tonight, actually. I hope you don't mind - the deadline was so close in the end, that I had to finish them during the painting classes. A lot of the kids already know the story."

Fia's shoulder dropped a little in relief. She always imagined an empty room the night before these things, and it was reassuring to think that someone might come.

"No, it's a good idea. I always panic no-one is going to show up; hopefully we get a handful of people at least."

And then it was time to wait. In the end there was more than a handful of people, the shop floor was soon crowded, and Fia's hand soon began to cramp as she signed copies for the families that queued to see her. She greeted people and wrote her name over and over, until a small hand pulled at her knee, and when she looked down she saw Michael himself, staring up at her and pointing.

"I think he wants you to read to him," a musical voice said from the front of the table. "I've told him you don't have time for that today, but maybe on another occasion?"

Fia looked up into the eyes of an older woman, very stylishly dressed with her hair pulled back into a smooth bun. "Hello, it's nice to meet you," she said in confusion.

"It's wonderful to meet you, too. I'm Michael's grandmother - we're lucky enough to have him come and live with us, did you know? And we're over the moon to have him. My husband cried."

"I did not," said the man that stood next to her. "Don't believe a word she says."

His wife laughed at him, and it had a sound like tinkling bells. "He did, I assure you. Anyway, we had to come - Michael's told us all about the other story you've read to him, and we knew how much he'd love it here today. If you have some free time to spend with him, just let us know. We're trying to keep his life as consistent as possible."

Michael was climbing onto her lap now, and making himself at home. He pulled a copy of her book towards him, chattering to himself as he turned the pages.

"Do you trust me with him? You don't know me," she said.

"Of course, we absolutely do. We've heard all about you from our nephew Joel," Michael's grandmother said. "He's very complimentary; I've never heard him describe any woman the way he talks

259

about you."

"That's another reason we're here," said her husband, helpfully. "Never misses a chance to be nosy, does my wife. We wanted to welcome you to the family-"

"- As Michael's friend," his wife cut in. "Of course. We're here for him." She accepted the book that Fia signed for her. "Come on, little man. You've seen your friend, and we're holding up the line. We'll go for an ice-cream, yes? And you can see your Auntie another day."

"I'm not -" said Fia, but it was too late. The strange little family were heading for the exit.

Fia watched the little shadow of Michael toddle out of the bookstore in between his grandparents, and smiled. It was wonderful to see him so happy, but then the next person stepped forwards in the line and she didn't have any more time to think about it. She asked him about the dedication that he wanted, and wrote it on the flyleaf, continuing her work until the queue began to dwindle. The last couple left just as the winter sky grew dark, congratulating Fia on her latest work on their way.

"We're just so glad you're publishing again." said the husband. "Our daughter has all your books."

"It looks a little different," said the wife, "But I love the pictures. We'll get used to this style in no time."

Fia thanked them, and waved Susie over to talk to them. She looked a little overwhelmed, and that was only to be expected. They both missed Paul at events like this, but even the customers were moving on.

She began to tidy the table, stacking the few books that didn't sell, signing a few extra copies to leave at the bookstore. She jumped when a copy was dropped in front of her face.

"Louella?" she blinked up at her. "When did you get here?"

"Did you think I would miss my best friend's book launch? I don't think so. I had to sit through all those dumb practice stories you wrote in that spiral notebook in kindergarten; I've earned a bit of glamour. Sign it for me, please. Susie's already done it."

Fia considered it. "Have you already paid for it?"

"Of course not; I refuse to introduce money into a friendship. I shall swap for it instead."

Another thump onto the table. A black box file landed next to the children's book. It was instantly recognisable as one from her offices – a priority case, like the last one. Fia had a slight case of déjà vu.

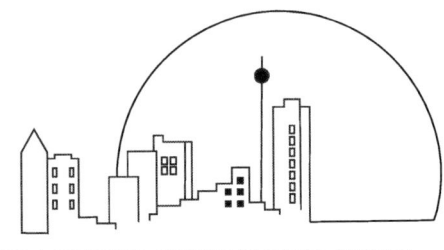

CHAPTER TWENTY-FIVE

"What's this?" Fia asked in surprise.

"You have a lot of unnecessary questions. Find out for yourself. But-" Louella slammed her hand down on the lid to prevent Fia opening it, "You can't look inside it until you've signed the book. Let's keep our accounts current, shall we?"

Fia grinned, and signed the book. She made the signature extra curly, so it took up the entire inside cover.

"Thank you. Here you go." Louella removed her arm. "Make of this what you will – but Fia, he put a lot of time into this, so don't be too angry with him. He's working himself to death at the moment. Also, it's his birthday today. Be kind."

"I'm always kind," Fia objected.

"I love you, but we all know that isn't always true."

Charly was motioning her away; Louella went to join her. The bookstore lights dimmed, and the sign was switched to 'closed'. Everyone began to take the posters down from the walls, but Fia sat and stared at the black box. She opened it. The paperwork inside was finely-written, and she only understood it well because she'd worked in the offices.

It was a legal case to return the rights of her children's book - the one with half the illustrations drawn by her brother; the story she'd read to Michael under the table at work. When she reached the final page, she saw that Joel Bard had succeeded where her agent had failed. She owned all the rights to it again - all she had to do was sign the contract on the final page, and return it to him to be submitted.

Her eyes filled with hot tears. "I'm going out," she said abruptly. "I've got something that needs finishing up."

Susie made complaining noises, but Louella shushed her. "Go on then," she encouraged, balancing on a chair to un-pin the top corner of a poster from the wall. "We've got this covered. Have fun."

The sun had set completely before Fia pulled

her Micra into the staff car park at JD Bard Associates, and parked next to the shiny Mercedes she found there. They didn't look too terrible sitting next to each other, she supposed. Not once you got used to it. She found the all-access pass inside her handbag where she'd left it, and scanned it on the side door. It still let her in, and that was unlikely to be an oversight. Tony was too organised with the security for that.

Hoping that this was a sign she was wanted, Fia wandered the corridors of the high-rise, her feet taking her to all the places that she'd spent time with Joel Bard in the past. The plastic bag she carried grew heavier and heavier the further she went, but he wasn't on the seventh floor, or in any of the meeting rooms. The kitchens were also empty, and she didn't bump into him a single time that she got into the elevator. After an hour of reminiscing, she remembered that there was one place left to try. He was most likely in the penthouse office, still wading through the paper trail of his cousin's awful legacy here, and trying to piece the business back together.

And there he was. Asleep at the desk, his sleeves rolled up and his jacket on the floor. Louella was right, he couldn't have stopped working at all over the past few weeks. Fia hesitated, and drew the bakery box from the plastic bag. She took out the cake she'd bought on the way.

She lit the candles and flicked the light switch off. The small flickering flames threw small shadows around the room as she began to sing softly.

"Happy birthday to you, happy birthday to you..."

The cake illuminated the dark shadows under his eyes as he slept. When had he last had a good night's sleep - when had he last eaten anything? He stirred as she grew closer to him, and his eyes opened, blinking in the light of the flames.

She knelt down and held out the cake firmly in both of her hands. He blew out the candles, and they were together in the darkness. The smoke from it wound its way through her hair, reminding her of childhood parties, and midnight vigils. He just sat looking at her, eyes wide and vulnerable. She'd never seen this expression on his face before, and for a moment she didn't know what to do.

Then she suddenly did. She lifted the cake upwards, pushing it towards him, resting it against his lips.

"Bite it," she said.

He just looked at her for another minute, and then did as he was told. He opened his mouth and bit down through the thick frosting, into the cake. Humming around the mouthful, he relaxed and closed his eyes as he swallowed. She watched his throat move before she twisted the plate and offered up another layer, tapping him gently on his lower lip once more.

"Again," she said.

He bit down again. Crumbs fell from his mouth and sprinkled over her blouse before tumbling down between her breasts. There was a ghost of a smile on his face then, and his shoulders shook slightly. She couldn't remember the last time he'd laughed.

"Sorry," he murmured, and attempted to dust them away for her until his hand snagged on something. He hooked one finger through the chain around her neck and pulled. The fine links swam over his knuckle until the 'F' snagged against his wrist, and the silver pulled tight. He lifted it up, turning it over to read it in the dim light.

"F?" he whispered, tracing the shape of it.

"Fia," she whispered back.

"Ah." He placed it back gently between her breasts, blowing lightly downwards to straighten the chain. Fia could feel her nipples furl into tight little buds. "Hello Fia," he said at last. "I'm Joel. It's a pleasure."

And he kissed her. He tasted like buttercream, and chocolate. The sweetness of it slid down her throat as he eased back, pressing tiny feather-light kisses to the corner of her mouth.

This was different from before, this was

gentle. He cupped his hands lightly beneath her chin, and swept his thumbs over her cheeks. She felt the tacky sugar trail that his touch left behind.

"And how about you, Fia?" he asked, tipping her head back and leaving a trail of chocolate mouth prints down the side of her neck. "Are you hungry too?"

"I-" He reached her collar bone, and she couldn't continue.

"Do you want cake, or do you want me?" he asked. "Both offers are on the table at this point."

Fia almost lost her hold on the cake, and Joel took it from her, digging one hand into it and twisting before carelessly dropping it onto the floor.

"Understood," he said, putting his fingers into her mouth. "Suck, please."

She did. The cake was delicious and she ate it all, licking his knuckles clean as he picked her up and placed her on his desk, pushing her legs apart. And then there were trails of sugar on her thighs as he pushed her skirt up, and the desk drawer was open and Joel held a condom wrapper between his fingers.

Fia licked his neck as he bent forward and fumbled with the fastenings on his trousers, giving him his own line of frosting to match her own. He hissed and stumbled for a moment before he slipped her panties to one side with his thumb. And then he was finally, finally inside her, and it had taken too long, and it was perfect.

Joel moved slowly at first, watching her reactions and letting her learn the shape of him.

"You've made me so hard," he said. "Nothing fixes it. I need-" but then he couldn't find the words and so Fia shushed him, and he just moved in earnest, fast and quick until she came around him in slippery tremors and he followed her three thrusts later.

"I never expected that," said Fia. She was sitting on the floor with her head on Joel's shoulder. He hummed lightly at her and continued to run his index finger absent-mindedly through the cake on the floor, occasionally offering it to her so she could lick it clean.

"You mean you didn't come here to be my birthday present?" his lips quirked.

"Not that." She scooped up some chocolate of her own and tapped it onto his nose. "I never thought I'd meet a speechless Joel Bard. Aren't you known for never running out of words?"

"This isn't the first time you've stopped me talking. You're going to ruin my reputation, I can tell."

Yes, he was right. His speech, of course. Fia thought about Joel, and his reputation. She saw the open drawer, and her smile vanished.

"Ah no, don't regret this, please. I didn't

mean it."

"You have condoms in your office?" This was a mistake. She was obviously just one woman in a long line. She stiffened.

But Joel just grinned, and pulled her into his arms. "Fia, Fia. I'm glad I'm not the only one whose brain isn't functioning now. And no, I don't have any in my office at all – I don't make a habit of this at work. You are the only one I want, I promise."

"But..."

"Look around you, woman. This is Darby's office."

Fia took in the scattered office supplies, the scuffed table and the cake that covered most of the floor. Her eyes widened. "Oh yes, so it is," she said.

Neither of them could contain their laughter. Fia was cheerful until she saw the screen of his laptop, and pulled it close to read it. Joel didn't make a move to stop her. She had access to everything, now. Her heart froze when she saw the list of court dates. Joel was fighting a long battle, and he'd been alone.

"I thought Darby would be too concerned with his reputation," he said dryly. "I really didn't think he'd fight me in court. This will damage the company. We need it over and done with as soon as possible."

"Do you think he will win?" asked Fia.

"No. I'm better at this than he is. He knows

269

that; he just wants to tank our reputation."

Fia huffed, and allowed him to suck some chocolate curls from her shoulder. "I can help," she said.

"You are helping," he murmured, nuzzling at her neck.

"I'm the one he falsely accused. I'm a witness to his confession."

He paused in his actions, then. "No. Don't get involved. You have your own career to think about."

"You've helped me. I need to repay the favour..."

"No."

"I'll ask the board members, then. I'm sure they'll agree with me."

"I'd hate to see you questioned. I won't see you on the stand."

"It will be fine, don't worry," said Fia. "One day this will all be sorted out, and we can go away for a while. A holiday far away from all of this..." She ran her fingers through his hair. "Maybe we could go sailing together, on your boat. Just the two of us. If a client wants you, they'll have to swim to get to you."

"Ah. I thought you'd like the yacht," said Joel. "I admit, I was trying to impress you then."

"Manipulator," she said.

"It's in the job description." Joel held her close. "You don't need to thank me. I helped you with your book because I wanted to, not so you would owe me something. I wanted everyone to see how hard you'd worked... and how talented you are."

"I'll testify," said Fia firmly. "Because you're mine, and I want to help."

The grip around her tightened so much, that for a minute Fia wondered if she'd ever be able to breathe again.

"Understood," he said. "I won't argue with you."

"Don't make promises you can't keep," said Fia. "It doesn't suit you."

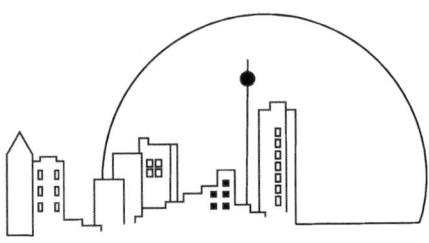

EPILOGUE

Joel's boat was just like he was on the outside,
carefully crafted from hard lines and shiny surfaces.
He'd taken Fia to see it one morning, driving her in
that damn Mercedes all the way down the centre of
the canyon that cradled the City, until she could see
the ocean in the distance. They arrived at a small
harbour, walking along the edge of it until they
reached all the luxury yachts at the far end.

Of course, he's got one of these super yacht
things, she thought, it couldn't be a cute little boat,
like the ones she'd wanted when she was younger. Fia
was beginning to worry that Joel Bard had serious
taste issues.

"Impossible," he told her. "I like you, don't
I?"

He was also unanswerable, as always. Fia stepped on board, managing to climb the ladder easily in her tennis shoes – perhaps he wouldn't have suited a woman in heels, after all. Joel helped her over the side and began to point out the yacht's features anxiously, as though he was really concerned about her opinion of it.

"I can barely see the damage on the side of it, since the repairs – that's one of the reasons I wanted to come down today," he told her. "You can't see a mark on it, can you? And of course, it's very quiet around here at the moment. It's the cold weather; I'll bring you here in the summer, and you'll enjoy it a lot more. It gets livelier then."

Fia looked up at the cliffs, all bright edges in the cold air, and breathed in the icy wind that came from the ocean, out beyond the walls of the harbour. It was beautiful here, and quiet.

"I think it's perfect like this," she said. "Just us, and the boat."

Then there was a thump from the other side of it. Fia followed the sound, and her eyes widened as she saw a familiar face on the other side of the deck. The little figure of Michael began to run towards her, waving a toy in her direction.

"Hey, little man, no running on the boat," Joel admonished him, sweeping him up into his arms as he almost tripped over. "If you go over the side, I'm going to have to explain myself to your grandparents, and I'll never survive it. Your grandmother could knock out an ox."

"How did he get here?"

"Michael here came with Uncle Tony; he's showing him how to catch a crab," said Joel seriously. "It's an important skill to learn. How many have you caught, Michael?"

The little boy solemnly held up three fingers, and tugged at Fia's jumper, inviting her to come and see them for herself – Uncle Tony was holding the bucket, and they were hoping for a fourth one soon. Joel shook his head at him.

"She'll come and see them in a minute, she's spending time with Uncle Joel at the moment, and he hasn't seen her for long enough yet."

Fia had been away on tour, promoting her book around the country, and she'd only arrived back in the City late the night before. Her agent had squeezed in as many visits as she could, and Fia felt as though her feet hadn't touched the ground for seven days. She had a small feeling this was why Joel had insisted on taking her out of the City for the day.

Her agent had maintained that it wasn't her fault; she would have spaced things out more evenly if Fia hadn't insisted on staying in the City until Darby's court case was over and done with, and Joel was the sole owner of JD Bard Associates. They kept the D in the name, but that was the only association that Darby would have with the company from now on. The last that she'd heard, he'd moved abroad and persuaded his young wife to go with him.

"You saw me all the way over here in the car," she protested, beginning to follow Michael back to his fishing station. "You can do without me for ten minutes - I've only been away a week!"

Joel just hooked an arm around her, holding her firmly in place. "And a week was long enough, thank you very much. Now, come and see the rest of the boat before we have some lunch. You haven't seen below deck yet."

Tony took Michael home in the early afternoon, with promises that he could visit again another day. The little boy stuck to him like glue, and it was obvious that he was becoming a second father to him. But Joel stayed there all day with Fia, until the sun set over the ocean and the cold chilled her skin, sipping wine made in the vineyards she could see on the shoreline as the boat gently rose and fell on the tamed waves of the harbour.

Eventually she began to fall asleep, and he suggested that they go back to the City. She said goodbye to the ocean as they walked back towards the car.

The houses that hugged the cliff faces were

beautifully kept, and Fia watched them pass by through the window with interest. She didn't even miss all the tiny multi-coloured fairy lights that had scattered across them, which had been carefully taken down by the owners after the New Year, and packed away in boxes waiting for the next holiday season.

"Do you like them?" Joel asked her, following her path of vision as they waited at the traffic lights. "I'll buy one, if you like. We could move into it, and you could look down on all of this chaos from above." He gestured at the roads around them, crowded with people and cars; the shoppers and the tourists, the dog leads twisting around the legs of pedestrians as they tried to fight through the wave of humanity.

Fia smiled, and leaned back against the cool leather of her seat, one step away from it all in the conditioned air of the car. "No, thank you. I like staying at your apartment, for now. I won't be there for long, anyway." '

The pipes had burst in the ceiling, and her tiny flat was flooded. She'd been staying with Joel at his apartment for the last two weeks, and was just waiting for the repairs to be finished. Now that she thought about it, it was taking a long time for her landlord to get the work done.

"Okay," was Joel's only reply, as he turned the car towards the financial district, and his home.

"There's no rush, I like it when you stay with me."

A horrible thought entered her head then, that he had delayed the repairs, and she wondered whether she should blame him for the unnaturally long time it was taking. Didn't he know most of the contractors in the City?

She pulled her mobile phone from her coat pocket. "Maybe I should just give my landlord a ring, and check for any updates. Or we could call in at my flat on our way? I'm worried about how long it's taking."

Joel Bard changed lanes quickly, barely signalling. A car horn sounded behind them, and they missed the exit that would take them towards the older, more run-down side of town that Fia lived in.

"Another day," he said airily. "I've got some work to do when we get back – I don't want to be home too late."

Home. He used that word a lot, now. They might have to have a conversation about it soon. Fia sighed, and went back to looking out of the window.

She showered while he looked over some files on the sofa, the warm water running over her shoulders and steaming up the glass of the divider, the sea salt diluting from her skin and washing away down the drain. A creaking sound came from the doorway, and when Fia wiped some of the steam from the glass, she saw that Joel had opened the bathroom door as he'd fetched a whiskey. He wanted to watch her shower while he worked. She smiled, and worked another palmful of shampoo into her hair, and he sat back down on the sofa, toasting her with his glass as he removed his tie.

Fia went to bed early; the sea air and the early start had caught up with her. Joel finished working on his case first, and it wasn't the first time that she was reminded just how much of a workaholic he was. Still, she was no different when a writing deadline loomed. He eventually came into the bedroom to undress, and Fia pushed herself up on one elbow to watch him.

He unbuttoned the cuffs on his starched shirt, and popped the collar before undoing the button near his throat. She gestured him closer, and he sat on the end of the bed as she slowly undid the rest of them, and pushed it from his shoulders.

"If you're going to do that, then I deserve a turn," he said, slipping the straps of her nightgown from her shoulders, the satin of it dropping to her lap, and pooling around her navel.

It was still so new, seeing him naked. Fia stripped him slowly, cataloguing all the warm skin that she uncovered, skin that had defied the winter and kept its sun-kissed glow. She was as pale as a ghost by comparison. She rested her forearm next to his; hers snow-white and smooth, his dark, with a dusting of hair that caught between her knuckles as she clasped his wrist to remove his watch for him.

He laughed, and pulled her onto his lap, conveniently leaving her nightgown behind on the bed, kissing her neck as he wrapped them both beneath the sheets. The soft duvet puddled around them as he gripped her jaw to turn her head and kissed her, his tongue licking gently at her lips before he buried it in her mouth.

She wanted to look at him, but he stayed behind her, shifting to bite gently between her shoulder blades as he entered her, moving quickly until he was flush against her spine, not able to wait any longer. There wasn't enough warning - it was too hard, she was stretched too far around the thickness of it, and Fia twitched forwards, sliding him out of her half-way, buying herself a moment to get used to him. He hesitated for a breath before moving more slowly, taking his time.

"After all," he whispered, "We've got all night. I can manage all night."

He hooked an arm around her stomach, holding her warm and tight, and so flat against him that she couldn't move at all, grinding up into her as he increased his movements and her thighs began to tingle, and she began to lose her breath. The sheet was rucking up beneath her, the wrinkles of it imprinting on her skin. She was cocooned, warm, safe. They were wrapped up together with all the time in the world.

She only came twice before he followed her; her muscles squeezing him so violently the second time that he cursed, his thrusts slowing down, his hands in her hair pulling just a little too hard as he lost control.

"Give me a minute," he said, pulling out of her. "Then we can do it again. I've missed you."

"I won't go away again until the spring," Fia replied. "If I stay with you until then, will you slow down a bit?"

"Probably not, to be honest." He considered it for a moment, pouring a glass of water for her from the carafe beside the bed. She drank it as he opened the drawer there, and removed something from it. "You'll stay in this apartment? You won't move back home?"

"I'll stay with you. But I'll need to bring some more things over from my flat – will that bother you?"

Joel looked up, hugging her close to him from behind as they both sat against the pillows in the bed, the clock beside them counting away the hours in the middle of the night.

"More things like that?" he asked, pointing at the large canvas that hung on the wall opposite the bed. "I like these things; they're colourful. Bring as many as you like. I'll come with you to help you choose."

Fia looked at the painting of the evening star, and the sunset clouds around it, the exact colour of the ones she'd seen out to sea earlier that evening. The thought that Paul might have been there made her smile – he'd always had such a memory for colours. The baby dragons that gambolled through them stood out from it like little jewels, the only pop of bright colour in the white and cream of the apartment. It was just made to be hung in this space.

"I can manage that," she said, leaning back into him.

His thumbs massaged at her throat, before she felt him fiddling with the clasp of her 'F' necklace. Her hand went up to protect it at once, from habit, and he tutted at her as he gently undid her fingers.

"It's alright. This is temporary," he assured her as she felt something cold slip onto the chain, falling down to meet the letter at the bottom point of the necklace. He fastened it closed again immediately.

She picked it up, and it sparkled in the light. A diamond ring, in a beautiful setting – the shape of a star. Fia gave him a questioning look over her shoulder. Joel gently removed it from her grip and released the chain, the 'F' and the ring nestling between her breasts and hidden in her cleavage once more.

"Here, keep it there for now," he advised her,

with all the gravitas of a lawyer speaking to a naughty client. "No-one will know about it unless you want them to. But when you're ready, that's going on your finger, I can promise you that."

Fia just tipped up a smile at him, and nodded a resigned yes. Sometimes she just had to let him win, after all.

ALSO BY POPPY BREEZE

CITY ROMANCE BOOKS:

Overruled – City Romance Book One.

Bloom – City Romance Book Two.

Coming in 2024:

Hotwire – City Romance Book Three.

Simmer – City Romance Book Four.

ABOUT THE AUTHOR

Poppy Breeze lives among the bright lights of London, which is nothing like the City of her imagination. She believes in strong women who can fight for themselves, and that although surviving romance can be tricky, everyone deserves a happy-ever-after. Eventually. If all else fails, she recommends a hot cup of tea.

Made in United States
Orlando, FL
02 February 2026